21st March – 20th April

Loved ones will be making many demands on you this week. It's essential that you stand up for yourself. A series of mysterious and worrying events will increase family tensions. Try to stay calm. An over-emotional response will only make things worse.

Also available in this series

MARIA PALMER

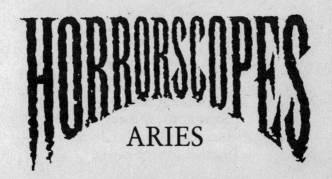

HORRORSCOPES

ARIES

BLOOD STORM

MAMMOTH

First published in Great Britain 1995
by Mammoth, an imprint of Reed Consumer Books Ltd
Michelin House, 81 Fulham Road, London SW3 6RB
and Auckland, Melbourne, Singapore and Toronto

Horrorscopes is a trademark of Reed International Books Ltd

ISBN 0 7497 1860 9

A CIP catalogue record for this title
is available from the British Library

Printed in Great Britain
by Cox & Wyman Ltd, Reading, Berkshire

ONE

Head down against the driving rain, Kate Carter cycled along the busy high road. She swerved into the kerb as an overtaking bus showered her with spray.

Doggedly she rode on homewards, wondering why she felt so low. Had it been that horoscope? She'd borrowed some glossy magazine to read when rain kept them stuck indoors during break. Inevitably it had a horoscope page. Just as inevitably, Kate, who didn't believe in horoscopes in the least, had turned to Aries. Immediately she wished she hadn't. Most horoscopes seemed to be vague and cheerful. 'Good news, and romantic interest from a handsome stranger.' Not Aries.

Aries had been as worrying as it was specific. 'Loved ones will be making many demands on you this week. It's essential that you stand up for yourself. A series of mysterious and worrying events will increase family tensions. Stay calm — an over-emotional response will only make things worse . . .'

They must put a bad one in every week to make the others look good, decided Kate. This week had been Aries' turn. But she was unhappy about it all the same. She told herself not to be silly. After all, it was Friday, no more school, the weekend ahead. But, she still had a bad feeling, as if something terrible was hanging over her – over all the family.

Over both her families.

Kate turned out of the high street and cycled up the steep tree-lined street where they lived. Number 13 was half-way up on the right, a big old terraced house with a short flight of steps leading up to the front door. Two pillars flanked the door itself, each bearing an enormous stone flower-pot. Her father said the builder must have had delusions of baronial grandeur.

The house had actually been numbered 11A when they bought it but her father, who was defiantly unsuperstitious, had restored the real number. Kate always claimed she wasn't superstitious either, but the change had worried her a bit. She was secretly afraid it might bring them bad luck.

Locking her bike in the little shed at the side of the house, Kate fished out her key.

The hall was dark and silent. 'Hello!' she yelled hopefully. 'Anyone home?' There was no reply. Susan must be out somewhere with Chrissie.

As she hung up her wet coat, Kate thought she was lucky really. She got on pretty well with her new stepmother. What an old-fashioned fairy-tale word that was. It didn't seem to fit Susan who was young, fair-headed and pretty, much more like the traditional princess.

If you were looking for a wicked stepmother, her real mother Maggie – black-haired, sharp-tongued with a hell of a temper – would be much better casting. Which only went to show, real life is nothing like fairy-tales.

Kate took after her mother in looks and in temper. Before the divorce they'd fought like a couple of cats – Kilkenny cats, Dad said, whatever they were. Kate still missed her mother and wondered if she was as happy as she pretended to be. One thing about Maggie, she always put up a good front.

Turning on lights everywhere to cheer herself up, Kate went into the kitchen and put on the kettle. Tea and a jam sandwich was what she needed. She caught sight of herself in the mirror over the sink, thin-faced, dark-haired, wrapped in a black polo-neck sweater.

Kate sighed. Ah yes, the sweater; late for school, with nothing warm to wear on such a rotten day, she'd grabbed the black sweater from her brother Jon's bed. Although he was two years younger, they were much the same size. She'd hoped to be out of the house before he noticed, but he'd spotted it as she was leaving. There'd been a nasty scene.

Sometimes Kate thought young Jon was in danger of turning into an all-time nerd. Bright and bespectacled, obsessively neat and tidy, he had a number of weird interests, everything from UFOs to mysticism, ESP and the occult. He spent most of his time in his room hunched over a computer keyboard. He hated having his things 'interfered with' as he put it. His room was forbidden territory to the rest of the family.

He'd been really nasty about the sweater, and Kate had resented it, especially since she'd been totally in the wrong. 'Pompous little prig,' she muttered. Still, she'd better do the right thing.

She ran up the stairs to her room, found the clean sweater she hadn't had time to look for this morning, and changed into it. Folding Jon's sweater over her arm, she headed for his room. She'd put his rotten sweater back where she'd found it. He could like it or lump it, it was all the apology he was going to get.

She opened the door to Jon's room, stepped inside and then froze, looking around her in utter astonishment.

The room had been totally wrecked. Clothes, books, records, CDs, tapes, computer game cartridges, were scattered all over the room. For a moment Kate just stood there open-mouthed. On the rare occasions she'd been permitted a glimpse inside, Jon's room had always been immaculate. There was something shocking in seeing it in such a state. It looked sinister, almost unnatural. It was like seeing someone covered with blood and grime after a terrible accident. It was as if Jon himself had been attacked. Savagely attacked, by someone who really hated him.

Kate felt a stab of unreasoning fear and she had a sudden urge to get out of there. Tossing Jon's sweater on the ruined bed she stepped back into the corridor, slamming the door behind her – just as Jon came up the stairs.

He stopped on the top step, glaring suspiciously at her.

'What were you doing in my room?'

Kate swallowed. She didn't seem able to answer. As Jon pushed past her she croaked, 'Jon, don't . . .'

Jon flung open the door of his room, and then froze, exactly as Kate had done moments before. Somehow it seemed weirdly funny. To her horror Kate heard herself giggling nervously.

She followed him into her room. 'Jon, listen . . .'

He turned round to face her. 'You lousy bitch!'

The mild obscenity was particularly shocking coming from Jon.

Kate heard the front door open and Susan's voice calling, 'We're back! Anyone home?' She was too preoccupied to answer.

Jon snatched up the black sweater from the bed. 'It was all over this, wasn't it? All because I gave you a hard time when you stole it this morning.'

Trust him to say 'stole', thought Kate. He always has to make things sound worse. She could feel her own temper rising.

'I didn't steal your rotten sweater, I borrowed it. And I didn't do all this either.'

'Come off it! I just caught you coming out of my room, didn't I? You were laughing about it.'

'I wasn't laughing,' said Kate helplessly.

Jon was looking furiously around the room. 'You came in and did all this to get your own back. Just because your room's a pigsty you made mine look the same . . .'

Kate felt a sudden stab of anger. Unkind though it was, there was an uncomfortable amount of truth in the pigsty charge. Remembering the horoscope, she tried to keep calm.

'Jon, please, listen . . .'

He stepped forward and slapped her hard across the face.

There was no question of calmness after that. Kate wasn't the sort of girl to scream and faint when she was attacked. There had been one or two nasty incidents on the local common and her school had started self-defence classes.

Ignoring the pain in her blazing cheek, she stepped forward and jabbed Jon hard under the nose with the heel of her hand.

'Don't you use your fists young ladies,' said the instructor, a fatherly middle-aged ex-Marine. 'Fists is fragile, like a bag of chicken bones. Heel of the hand is best.'

Jon staggered back, a spray of bright red blood gushing from his nose. His nose had always been tender, Kate remembered. He'd suffered a lot from nose bleeds when he was little.

Jon clutched at his face with both hands, and brought them away smeared with blood. Hands and face red, he looked like something from a horror film. Suddenly he hurled himself on Kate, gripping her around the throat with bloody fingers.

Kate struggled wildly but the usually-weedy Jon seemed to have the strength of anger – or

6

was it madness? She felt herself choking as his grip tightened around her throat. He's going to kill me, she thought. My own brother's going to kill me. There was a roaring in her ears and things started going black.

Somewhere she heard the instructor's voice. '*To break a stranglehold, clasp your own two hands together and bring them up hard between those of the attacker . . .*'

She did it, knocking Jon's hands apart. Then she brought her knee up, hard.

'*Use your bony bits, knees and elbows – and remember, hard against soft.*'

Jon staggered back gasping, and Kate became aware that Susan was in the doorway. Chrissie was peering from behind her, dark eyes enormous.

'Stop it both of you!' screamed Susan.

Jon was berserk with rage. Recovering, he hurled himself on Kate, knocking her off her feet. They rolled over and over on the floor. Kate wasn't frightened, just filled with sudden fury. She was thinking of some of the other things she'd been taught, the dangerous moves you were only supposed to use if your own life was in danger. Still, Jon had started it, hadn't he? He was asking for it. If she could just get a good choke-hold, she'd show him what it felt like to be really throttled . . .

She heard Susan shouting and footsteps thundering up the stairs. A big hand gripped her shoulder painfully hard, hauling her to her feet. The newcomer's other hand was holding Jon.

The hands shook them both till their teeth rattled and then flung them apart.

Dad was back, and he wasn't pleased.

Jack Carter was a big man with dark skin, curly black hair, and a power-house of a personality. In a good mood he gave off cheerfulness and confidence like a warm fire. But the mood could switch with alarming suddenness to gloom and despair, or to black, terrifying rage. He was angry now – you could feel the anger radiating off him in waves.

He looked around the wrecked room, at his battered son and daughter, at his second wife and his new stepdaughter and said, 'Well?'

Nobody moved or spoke. Nobody dared.

In a voice that rattled the window panes Jack said, 'I've had a bad day at the office. Difficult. Frustrating. So since it's Friday I thought, the hell with it, I'll go home early, to the peace and comfort of my little family. And what do I find? I find I've walked into the middle of a video nasty.' His voice rose to a roar, '*Will someone please tell me what the hell is going on?*'

Jon and Kate were used to their father yelling, but they still found it pretty scary. He never actually hit them, but the force of his anger was frightening in itself. Susan and Chrissie were clearly terrified.

Jack saw their reaction and made an effort to control himself. He went over to Susan and put an arm around her shoulders, stroking Chrissie's hair with the other hand. 'Sorry, love, you must think you've married into a madhouse.'

Oh, sure, he'll calm down for them, thought Kate bitterly. He never did for us – or for Maggie.

'I don't know what happened,' said Susan. 'I took Chrissie out for a walk and when I came back they were fighting.' She looked at him helplessly.

Typical Susan, thought Kate. Still, it works. If he'd yelled at Mum like that she'd have said, 'How the hell am I supposed to know – they're your kids too, you sort it out!' Then they'd have been off on another ding-dong! She couldn't help smiling at the thought.

Unfortunately her father noticed and it set him off again. 'There's nothing to smirk at my girl. Maybe *you'd* like to tell me what this is all about?'

Before Kate could reply Jon screamed, 'It-was-her-she-stole-my-sweater-and-I-told-her-off-and-then-she-came-up-here-and-trashed-my-room-I-know-it-was-her-I-saw-her-coming-out!'

It came out all at once in a sort of hysterical gabble.

Jack Carter gave him an impatient look and said, 'Well, Kate?'

'I never touched his room!' said Kate angrily. She made an effort to keep calm. 'It's true I borrowed Jon's black sweater without asking. I got back from school first, took it off and went to Jon's room to return it. The room was like this when I opened the door. Jon turned up and saw me coming out of his room. He

9

went in himself, saw all this and thought I'd done it.'

'And who started the fight?'

Kate didn't say anything.

'Well?' snapped her father.

Jon said, 'I did. I was so angry I hit her.'

'Looks as if she gave you as good as she got,' said his father. He turned to Kate. 'You say you didn't trash the room?'

Kate resented the question – she'd *told* him, hadn't she?

'No I didn't.'

Jon was wiping his face with a handkerchief. 'Somebody did.'

Jack looked thoughtfully around the room. 'They certainly did, didn't they?'

Now he's being the Great Detective, thought Kate. Carter of the Yard is on the Case!

Her father turned to Jon. 'Anything stolen?'

Drying his hands and face, Jon gazed hopelessly at his scattered possessions. 'How can I tell with it all like this? Some CDs are gone I think, and a few of the computer game cartridges.'

'There you are,' said Jack. 'Kids!'

'What kids?' asked Kate.

'You know – kids. Vandals. Juvenile delinquents.'

Typical adult thinking, thought Kate. Blame the kids. Aloud she said, 'Teenagers crazed by sex, drugs and rock 'n' roll? Heavy metal fans? Train-spotters?'

Her father ignored her. 'Susan and Chrissie were out for a walk, you two weren't back from school, so the house was empty. Was the window left open like this?'

Jon nodded, and his father went over to the window and looked out. 'There you are then.' He pointed downwards. 'It's an easy climb up that drainpipe. Some local yob sees the open window, gets into the garden, shins up the pipe, climbs in and looks round for money. Doesn't find any, so he starts wrecking the room out of spite. Then he hears Kate come in, grabs what he can, and slides back down the drainpipe.'

'Are you going to all the police?' asked Kate.

He shook his head. 'No point.'

'But, Dad – '

'Remember last year when someone broke in and stole the video? We called the police then. They came round, asked a few questions, and what happened? Nothing! Didn't catch the burglar, didn't find the video. Waste of time.'

It seemed all wrong to Kate but she was too tired to argue. 'Maybe you're right.'

'Course I am,' said Jack. 'Now, let's all give Jon a hand clearing up, shall we?'

Jon shook his head. 'Easier if I do it, I know where everything goes.'

Jack and Susan and Chrissie went downstairs.

Kate hesitated in the doorway, looking at the skinny figure alone in the wrecked room. 'Sure you don't want any help?'

'No, I'll do it!'

'I really didn't wreck your room, you know.'

'All right, I believe you.' But he didn't.

'Sorry about the wallop on the hooter.'

11

Jon touched his swollen nose. 'Yeah, I owe you one for that. Now beat it and let me clear up.'

Jon slammed the door in her face and Kate went slowly downstairs. She didn't believe her father's drain-pipe-climbing delinquent theory. It just didn't feel right. But she knew she hadn't wrecked Jon's room . . .

Kate stopped for a moment, half-way down the stairs. She hadn't wrecked it – but she *had* thought about it. After the row at breakfast a picture of Jon's over-neat room had flashed through her mind, and she'd imagined reducing it to a shambles like her own. But she hadn't *done* it, Kate told herself fiercely. She'd gone straight out of the house.

At least, she thought she had. Maybe she'd had a mental lapse. Like the bloke in that horror story who kept waking up with blood on his hands and no idea where it had come from.

Maybe she'd done it without knowing . . .

Kate carried on down the stairs, wondering why she suddenly felt so afraid. It was the same irrational feeling she'd had earlier, cycling home. An unreasoning fear that something terrible was hanging over them all.

TWO

Jack poured more wine into his glass, and swigged it down with a shudder. 'Where'd you get this stuff?'

Susan looked worried. 'It was on special offer at the supermarket.'

He peered suspiciously at the label. 'Sicilian! I thought as much. It's the Mafia's revenge!' He poured another glass. Kate helped herself to another sausage and another dollop of mashed potatoes. 'I bet you'll be glad when it's finished!'

He gave her a mock-scowl. 'Not so much of your cheek, my girl. Ah well, it may be rotgut but it's all we can afford.'

'I know,' said Kate. ' "In these hard times . . ." '

It was an old music hall song and it had become the Carter family anthem.

Jack Carter was an architect. He'd gone into business for himself in the booming eighties and, like a lot of other people, he'd done very well. Clients had flowed in and money poured in with them. Kate had grown up in a carefree atmosphere of big houses, big cars and expensive foreign holidays. Her mother Maggie was a design consultant and she'd been successful as well. Then the recession struck.

According to Jack, architects were hit first and worst. 'Other businesses went into a gentle decline,' he said. 'The architect business shot straight over a cliff!'

Maggie's design business had folded almost immediately. Jack had to lay off his staff and move from a snazzy office block to a tiny office. He took on jobs he wouldn't have looked at in happier times. They'd had to sell their big new house and move to this shabby old house in an unfashionable part of town.

Jack's business had survived, just about. His marriage hadn't.

There'd always been fights, of course, right from the very beginning. Kate's earliest memory was of lying quaking in bed listening to her parents yelling at each other. She remembered her big brother Nick putting his arms around her when she cried.

'Don't worry,' Nick used to say. 'They'll make up by morning.'

Usually they had.

There'd been fights, but there'd been fun and laughter and love in the marriage as well. Then, as business got worse and worse, there were just the fights. The strain of Jack's business struggles had worsened his already unreliable temper. The whole family suffered. It was as if no one could do anything right.

One day Maggie had simply walked out on him. She said she could put up with Jack, and she could put up with being poor. The two together had been too much to bear.

Nick was at college by then. He'd never really got on with his father, taking his mother's side in the increasingly frequent family rows. He'd moved out as soon as he could, sharing a flat with some other students in the town. For quite a while there'd just been the three of them, Kate, Jon and their father.

It had been a very dodgy period. Jon was moody at the best of times, made worse by his mother leaving. Kate had fought like mad against getting pushed into the job of substitute mum. The house was in a state, there never seemed to be anything to eat. As for Jack Carter – it was like living with an unexploded bomb.

Gradually, they got themselves organised. Maggie's solicitor got in touch with Jack's solicitor and in time an agreed no-fault divorce came through.

Slowly but surely business started to pick up. Jack was able to take on extra staff, including a temporary secretary called Susan, divorced, with a little girl of her own. Six months after Susan joined the firm, she and Jack Carter were married.

As she looked around the silent dinner-table, Kate thought there was something to be said for the new arrangement. Susan was pretty much Maggie's opposite, which was probably why Jack had picked her. She tended to agree with him rather than talk back. (Maggie had *always* talked back.) Life was a lot quieter now that Nick and Maggie had gone . . .

Sometimes Kate felt it was too quiet. In the old days, with Jack, Maggie, Nick and Kate as well, all talking, laughing and arguing – and often fighting – things were noisy but never dull. The anger came out and exploded harmlessly, like fireworks. But now . . .

Nobody shouted or yelled these days except Jack, and even he had quietened down. But somehow Kate felt the anger in the family was still there, hidden under the new, smooth surface like a buried time-bomb.

Jon had always been quiet and he still was – particularly so tonight, when he was sulking. Susan never said very much, and little Chrissie never said anything at all. Small, slender and dark – apparently she took after Kevin, her father – with a cloud of black hair, Chrissie just *looked*, staring at everything with huge black eyes.

Chrissie didn't talk. Not couldn't, just didn't.

Apparently there'd been some fear at first that Chrissie was autistic, locked inside herself like the Dustin Hoffman character in *Rain Man*. However, after lots of tests, the experts at her special school had decided things weren't nearly that bad. After all, it wasn't as if Chrissie couldn't talk. She'd started talking quite normally when she was small. Then she'd suddenly stopped, around the time Susan's first marriage was breaking up. Given plenty of loving care, and a secure environment, said the experts, she'd simply grow out of it.

Kate found the brooding silence was getting

on her nerves. 'What's all this about having a bad day?' she asked. 'I thought the recession was over and we were all moving forward to the broad sunlit uplands of prosperity?'

Jack snorted. 'One step forwards, two steps back more like it. The Bellingham people are dragging their feet over that hotel complex. Problems with the finance.'

'They'll come through eventually though, won't they?' asked Susan. She still worked part-time in her husband's office so she knew what was going on.

'Oh yes, the deal's pretty solid. It's just the delay.'

'So what's knocked you out of your pram?' asked Kate.

'Apart from coming home to a prize-fight, you mean?'

Jon looked up quickly and scowled, but he didn't say anything. He hated his father's continual teasing.

'Before that,' she said firmly. 'You said you'd had a bad day and had decided to come home early.'

Jack glared and Kate started wishing she'd never asked.

'Well, if you must know . . .' He glanced at Susan and then looked away. 'I was waiting for a good time to tell you all, but I don't suppose there is one really. I had a phone call from Maggie this afternoon.'

Kate could actually *feel* Susan's tension. Maggie had disappeared from the scene after the separation. Soon after Jack's remarriage she'd turned up again. Now she had a good job with the town council and a flat in the best part of town. She looked smart and glamorous, very much the rising executive.

They all met up again from time to time – there were no problems about access or anything of that sort. Everyone was determined to be modern and civilised. But the meetings always felt a bit awkward, and gradually contacts had become more and more rare. Nick saw more of Maggie than anybody. He'd been very much on her side over the split.

Kate only saw her mother occasionally. Maggie was always saying, 'We must meet for coffee,' or 'Let's have lunch.' But somehow they didn't actually get together all that often. Kate told herself it was only natural for Maggie to be so busy, absorbed in her new life, her new career, and a succession of new boyfriends.

By now Kate had accepted the divorce. Maggie was her mother, nothing could alter that. But things had changed and they weren't going to change back. She had a feeling that Jon still found Maggie's leaving harder to take. Since he never mentioned her, it was hard to tell.

It was Susan who saw Maggie as a real problem. Kate suspected she thought of Maggie as impossibly glamorous, high-powered competition, who might some day decide to take Jack back again. Kate reckoned the only person who'd hate the idea more than Jack was Maggie herself – but there was no way to convince Susan.

Susan looked down at her plate. 'What did she want?'

'It was about Nick,' said Jack Carter disgustedly. 'Guess what?'

'He's failed his exams?' said Kate.

Her father stared at her in astonishment. 'Maggie phoned you as well?'

'No, but I know Nick.'

Jack shook his head. 'When I think how I sweated and struggled to get myself qualified, to get on . . .'

Kate knew it was true enough. Her father's parents had been hard up, and getting qualified, setting up his own business, had been a real struggle.

'Now everyone seems to expect to go to university and no one values it.'

'Not everybody, Dad,' said Kate firmly. 'But there are a lot more graduates – and a lot fewer jobs for them. Still, if Nick's only failed once he's not necessarily out on his ear for good, is he?'

'That's the really aggravating bit. Apparently he could re-take the exams if he wanted to, but he can't be bothered. He wants to chuck it all in, leave university. He told Maggie he'll still end up on the dole with a degree, so he might as well start now without one!'

'And what did Maggie want?' asked Kate. 'Apart from sharing the good news?'

'She wants me to talk some sense into him!'

'Are you going to try?'

'I suppose I shall have to,' said Jack grimly.

19

'Not that he'll pay any attention to me, he never does.' He started getting angry again. 'Of all the arrogant, bad-tempered, bullying louts . . .'

'Now who does that remind me of?' said Kate thoughtfully.

Her father jumped up and thumped the table with his fist, making plates and cutlery jump and jingle. 'Now see here – ' Chrissie winced and Susan looked horrified.

'I rest my case!' said Kate.

Jack sat down. 'All right, maybe Nick and I are too much alike to get on. What gets me is Maggie's attitude. He took her side when we split up, she sees far more of him than I do but as soon as Nick's in trouble, he's my responsibility!'

'I don't see that you and Nick having another blazing row will help things much,' said Kate. 'Why don't you let me talk to him first? I could go round and see him this evening, it's not far on the bike.'

'I'd be glad if you would,' said Jack Carter frankly. 'You're a good girl Kate, even though you are so cheeky!'

'Stops you getting above yourself,' said Kate.

'Right, let's get cleared up,' said her father. 'I've had enough of today. I want a few cans of beer, some nice mind-numbing telly and an early night.'

Susan took Chrissie upstairs for a bedtime story, Jon took out the rubbish, and Kate and her father cleared away and washed up.

'Are you going to do anything more about that business earlier?' said Kate.

'What business?'

'Jon's room being wrecked.'

'What do you expect me to do?'

'I still think you ought to call the police.'

'Not worth the trouble, love.'

'Maybe you're right . . .'

'That's not like you – agreeing with me!'

'I don't,' said Kate. 'I'm still not so sure it was some kid climbing in.'

'What else could it have been?'

'I don't know.'

Jack said, 'And look, let's have no more fighting between you and Jon. You're too big for that now. Besides, it all got a bit vicious.'

'He hit me first,' said Kate. 'But I'll forget it if he will.'

Jack looked round. 'Where's Jon got to anyway? He must have finished taking the rubbish out by now.'

'Maybe he's fallen in the dustbin. I'll check on my way out.'

'All right. Take care. Don't be back too late.'

Jack took a can of lager from the fridge and went off to the sitting room and the telly. Kate got her coat from the hall and went out. The bike shed was round the side of the house. As Kate came down the front steps she saw Jon coming out.

'Going somewhere?' she called.

Jon shook his head. 'I was looking for something in my saddlebag but it wasn't there.'

'I'm just off to see Nick. Want to come?'

'I still haven't finished clearing up my room.'

Kate hesitated. 'It really wasn't me, you know. Sorry about the punch-up.'

Jon rubbed the end of his nose. It was still a bit red. 'Well, I started it. Next time I'll pick on someone my own size.'

'No hard feelings?'

'We'll call it square, shall we?'

There was something very odd about Jon's manner. Odd and sly. He gave her a decidedly sinister smile and went back into the house.

Kate got her bike out and cycled slowly off. The S-shaped road curved downwards towards the busy high street. The final curve, just before the high street itself was the steepest bit of all. You had to watch yourself turning out of the steep side road into the main traffic stream.

It had stopped raining by now, but the road was still wet, covered with scattered leaves. Kate rode slowly, using both brakes on the curves. She was particularly careful as she turned into the last steep stretch, gripping both brake-levers hard. Suddenly she realised that something was wrong – the tyres felt soft. She was thinking about getting off and pumping them up when both brake-levers went slack. Kate squeezed hard on the handles, but nothing happened. The bike seemed to shoot forward of its own accord, hurtling downhill towards the roaring stream of traffic.

Kate saw a bus lumbering steadily down the high street. In a matter of seconds she'd be under its front wheels.

They say people see their whole lives flash

before them at times of great danger. What flashed before Kate's eyes was her life's end. She saw the bus bear down on her, felt the great wheels roll over her, crushing the life from her body. She saw the shocked face of the driver, the horrified looks of the passengers as they dragged her broken body from beneath the wheels. She saw the grief on her father's face as someone broke the news . . . Squeezing frantically on the useless brakes Kate hurtled towards certain death.

THREE

Kate was saved by a sudden realization – she couldn't stop, but she could still steer. She was going to smash into something all right – but it didn't have to be a bus.

She wrenched the handlebars round to the left, shot onto the pavement and straight into the low wall in front of a house. Her front wheel hit the wall, and the bike reared like a bucking bronco, sending Kate flying through the air. The house was guarded by a thick privet hedge and Kate smashed down into it like a bomb, the stiff prickly bushes breaking her fall. After thrashing around for a moment she extricated herself and struggled back onto the pavement. There were painful scratches on her face and hands, and her knee felt bruised, but apart from that everything seemed to be working.

She found that she was trembling with shock, and sat down on the wall till the shaking died down. After a few minutes, she felt better and got up to examine her bike. The front wheel was badly buckled but the rest of it seemed to be okay. She checked the brake-cables. Both of them, front and back, were dangling loose.

Lifting the front of her bike by the handlebars so it could run on the undamaged back wheel, Kate began plodding back towards home.

When she reached the house, she saw Jon standing on the front steps. He ran down as she stopped outside the house.

'What happened to you?'

Kate didn't reply. Was he really concerned? Or was there a mocking, triumphant tone in his voice? Grimly she shoved her battered bike into the shed, closing and padlocking the door. She turned to face Jon. 'Checking up to see how well it worked?'

'What do you mean?'

'My brakes failed and I came off.' She went close to him, looking hard at his face. 'Both brakes, Jon. Right on the steep bit, just before the high street. Funny that, isn't it?'

Jon didn't reply.

'And you were in the bike shed, weren't you? Just before I went out.'

He stared at her. 'Kate, you can't think – '

'Can't I? Just after that dust-up in the bedroom you said you still owed me one. When I was getting my bike out, you said we could call it square.' She grabbed him by the arm, squeezing hard enough to hurt. '*What did you do to square it?*' Jon pulled away. 'Get off, will you? I didn't do anything.'

A shadow blocked the light pouring from the front door. Their father's voice called, 'What's going on? Are you two fighting again?'

Kate let go of Jon. 'I skidded in the wet, came off my bike.'

Jack ran down the steps. 'Are you all right?'

'Just a few scratches and bruises. Front wheel's a write-off though.'

'Never mind that, just as long as you're okay.' Typically, his relief was followed by anger. 'The times I've told you kids to be careful. You go zooming down that hill . . .'

Kate looked at Jon's white face. 'I know, all my own fault. Save the telling off till later, will you?'

Suddenly Jon turned and ran back into the house.

'What's the matter with him?' demanded Jack.

'I think he was a bit upset by the accident.'

Her father shook his head. 'I just don't understand that boy. Sure you're all right?'

Susan started fussing when they got back into the house. It took Kate quite a while to persuade everyone that all she needed was a bath and an early night.

There was no sign of Jon, who'd disappeared into his room. But there was nothing unusual in that and with the fuss about Kate's accident no one even noticed.

Kate cleaned her cuts and bruises in the bath, wincing a bit at the sting of the hot water. She dabbed antiseptic on the cuts and put sticking plaster on the worst ones. Her knee was still a bit sore but otherwise she felt more or less okay.

Physically, at least.

She got into pyjamas and dressing gown, went down to the kitchen and made herself a mug of cocoa. She said goodnight to Jack and Susan, assured them all over again that she was really all right, and went upstairs to bed.

She went into her bedroom, switched on the light and put the cocoa on her bedside table. She stood thinking for a moment, wondering why she felt so uneasy. Reaction probably. On a sudden impulse she went over to the door and locked it. She lay on the bed with the light on and her mind went back over the events of the day.

The row at breakfast over the borrowed sweater.

Jon's trashed room and the vicious fight that had followed.

Jon coming out of the bike shed looking strange and furtive.

The accident.

Jon waiting on the steps of the house . . .

Kate replayed the events in her mind, again and again. All right, she'd borrowed the rotten sweater – but she hadn't trashed Jon's room.

But somebody had. Kate just didn't believe in her father's sneak thief theory.

The only other candidates were Susan or little Chrissie – and that seemed quite unbelievable. What possible motive could they have? It wasn't even their quarrel.

Of course, there is one other candidate, thought Kate. Jon himself. Suppose he trashed his own room in a fit of rage after the row at breakfast? Then hung about so he could catch me and use the wrecked room as an excuse to start a fight. When he came off worse, he fixed my brake-cables for revenge.

27

It didn't seem very likely. But then, every other idea seemed impossible too.

Kate realised how little she really knew Jon these days. He'd been a cheeky, lively little kid and they'd played and scrapped like any other brother and sister.

In his early teens Jon had changed more or less overnight. He'd become silent and withdrawn, with all kinds of weird interests. By the time the computer obsession had started, Nick and Kate, both lively and outgoing, had pretty well given up on him.

For all she knew, thought Kate, Jon could have been going quietly potty for years. He'd certainly taken the divorce harder than any of them. Maybe it had tipped him over the edge.

What is it they say? thought Kate. It's the quiet ones you have to watch out for! Whenever someone runs amok and chops up their entire family with a hatchet someone always says, 'Who'd have thought it? Such a nice *quiet* boy.'

She told herself she was being ridiculous. Things like that just didn't happen. Then she remembered that they did. There were cases in the paper or on the news. All those true crime programmes on telly. They were full of children murdering their parents – or brothers killing sisters.

Suddenly she heard a rattling sound. Someone was trying the handle of the locked bedroom door.

Kate sat bolt upright like a Jack-in-the-box, her heart pounding. 'Who is it?'

A voice called softly, 'It's me, Kate let me in.'
It was Jon.

He's waiting outside my door, thought Kate. But what with? An axe? A length of rope? Maybe just a pillow, that'd be nice and quiet.

The door handle rattled again and suddenly she felt afraid. 'Go away,' she shouted, her voice quavering a little. 'It's too late, we can talk tomorrow.'

'Kate please . . .'

'Clear off, or I'll yell for Dad. You can have a nice chat with him – about brake-cables!'

Silence. She heard footsteps shuffling away from her door.

I'm just being silly, Kate told herself. Jon might play some stupid trick, but he wouldn't try to hurt me, not really. Of course he wouldn't.

But she got up and checked that the door was securely locked. She wedged a chair behind the door as well, the back jammed under the door-knob.

It took her ages to get to sleep.

Next morning everything looked different. The rain had cleared up and sunshine streamed through the bedroom curtains. Kate felt a real twit when she had to climb out of bed, move the chair and unlock the door – she knew Susan would be bringing her a cup of tea.

Normality continued during the traditional Saturday morning bacon and egg breakfast with her father, Susan and Chrissie.

No sign of Jon, but then there never was on weekend mornings. He stayed up half the night huddled over his computer, seldom emerging till midday.

Jack finished off the last piece of toast. 'No after-effects from the crash?'

'Bit stiff, that's all. Nothing serious.'

'Better get that bike fixed – yes, all right, I'll pay. We could try and strap it on top of the car if you like.'

'Not worth the bother, I'll wheel it down to the bike shop.'

After breakfast Kate went down to the bike shed and pulled out the battered bike. At the sight of the buckled front wheel all her old fears flooded back. She relived that terrible moment when the brake-levers went suddenly slack and she was speeding helplessly towards the traffic. Suddenly, she was shaking and her legs felt weak. She sat down on the house wall and drew a few deep breaths. She got up and trundled the bike down the street.

The high street bike shop's long front window was filled with display bikes, and there were more bikes chained to stands on the pavement outside. There was everything from incredibly expensive mountain bikes with ninety-nine gears to sturdy roadsters with sit-up-and-beg handles and massive saddle-bags.

The Carter family were old and regular customers. Over the years they'd bought everything from toddlers' tricycles to Nick's first mountain bike. Kate could remember Jack and Maggie taking her there to buy her first two-wheeler – with training wheels!

She wheeled the bike up to the long counter and waited to be served. Saturday morning was always a busy time.

One of the assistants, a spiky-haired lad called Jason, was from Kate's school, working there as a Saturday job. Kate deliberately hung back till he was free and then wheeled the bike up to the counter.

'Morning, Jase. Got a patient for you.'

'Lo, Kate.' He peered over the counter at the bike. 'This has been in the wars.' He looked at her scratched face. 'You too!'

'Came off coming down the hill and went into a hedge.'

Jason tut-tutted. 'Careless! Not like you, Kate.' He came round from behind the counter and knelt to examine the bike. 'Front wheel's a write-off, no chance of straightening that. Have to put a new one in, do that in no time. Tyre's flat too, so's the back one. Want us to fix the flats as well?'

'Might as well. Every time I try to repair a puncture I make two more.'

Jason flipped a dangling brake-cable. 'This'll take a bit longer though. That what had you off?'

Kate nodded. 'Both brake-cables went when I was going down the hill.'

Jason looked curiously at her. 'Both of 'em went?'

'Both. At exactly the same time. What d'you reckon the chances of that are?'

'About a million to one. Must have been a real freak accident.'

'If it was an accident.'

'You reckon someone fixed it?'

'What do you think?'

Jason examined the frayed ends of the brake-cable. He moved to the back of the bike and examined the other snapped cable.

He squatted on his heels and looked up at her. 'For a start it should never have happened. The bike's not new – but it's not that old either. On the other hand the brake cables are definitely frayed, not cut.'

Kate felt a surge of relief. 'So it was an accident!'

Jase sucked his teeth. 'Well . . . not necessarily. Somebody could have filed the cables nearly through, leaving just a few strands, see? When they took the extra strain from going down a steep hill – ping!' He frowned. 'Even so . . .'

'What?'

'It'd be a hell of a job working out exactly how many strands to leave. Matter of luck, really. You say they both went at once?'

Kate nodded.

'Well, that's even more unlikely. What you'd expect, the back brake goes first, say, you bear down on the other and that goes as well. But fixing both to go together, to the second – I'd say that was pretty well impossible. You'd have to do a hell of a precise job.'

But Jon was precise, thought Kate. He was into meccano and models as well as computers, working steam engines, things like that. He'd have the tools for the job, the skill to carry it out.

'Could you prove these cables have been filed?' she asked.

Jason stood up. 'Well, *I* couldn't. Maybe a police lab could.'

'Will you do me a favour? When you take the broken cables off, don't throw them away, put them aside somewhere safe and hang on to them for me.'

'Okay.' Jason filled out a label with Kate's name and the job details and tied it to the handlebars. 'Be ready end of next week, all right? Thursday, maybe Friday.' He took hold of the bike to wheel it into the workroom. 'Kate?'

'What?'

'If you really think someone sabotaged your bike you should go to the police. I mean, this isn't just some silly trick like letting your tyres down. This is worked out, planned. We're talking attempted murder.'

FOUR

Kate's worries came down in a black cloud as she left the bike shop and turned into the bustling high street. She passed the police station on the corner with its traditional blue lamp and its equally traditional glass-fronted display case of fading notices about colorado beetles and rabid dogs.

There was a smudgy police artist portrait of a man wanted for a late-night murder on the Underground in the display case. For a moment it seemed to be Jon's face staring out at her. She thought about Jason's advice. Ought she to report what had happened? Or should she wait and see if Jon had another go?

Of course, if he had another go and was successful, she wouldn't be able to report anything . . .

On a sudden impulse Kate ran up the steps, pushed open the glass doors and went through into the reception area. Behind the counter, a shirt-sleeved young constable, who didn't look much older than she was herself, was interviewing a flustered looking middle-aged lady. The policeman was laboriously writing down details of a missing purse.

'My husband says I must have just left it somewhere,' the woman was saying. 'But I know I put it down on the kitchen table. Someone must have come into the house and stolen it, one of these walk-in thieves . . .'

The constable sighed. 'And at exactly what time did this occurrence take place?'

'Well, I'm not quite sure. I popped next door for morning coffee at about half-past ten – no, it must have been nearer eleven . . .'

It looked like being a long job. Suddenly Kate couldn't bear the idea of waiting. She turned and ran out of the stuffy little room and back down the steps. She could just imagine the look on that young policeman's face if she told him her story about snapping brake-cables.

'Had a right nutter in this morning,' he'd say later in the canteen. 'Thinks her brother's trying to murder her . . .'

Of course, when her mysteriously-dead body was found, he'd have to think again. He'd be sorry then.

Suddenly someone grabbed her by the arm. 'Gotcha!'

Kate swung round, ready to strike. The grabber was a large, scruffily-dressed, wild-looking young man with long hair and designer stuble.

She grinned and relaxed. 'Nick you idiot! What are you doing here?'

'Coming round to see you, strangely enough. Maggie phoned Dad this morning. He told her about the accident and she phoned me. Maggie's tied up so I thought I'd come round and make sure you were still in one piece. What were you doing coming out of the cop shop?'

Typical of Nick to rush round, thought Kate. For a moment she was tempted to tell him about her fears but she decided against it. He was quite likely to grab Jon and try to shake the truth out of him. Somehow Kate didn't think that would help much. If her suspicions of Jon were correct it might even be dangerous.

'I thought maybe I ought to report the accident,' she said. 'But I decided not to bother.'

Nick nodded approvingly. 'Quite right. Less you have to do with the Old Bill the better.'

Nick's past contacts with the police hadn't been too friendly. He was exactly the kind of teenager they viewed with automatic suspicion, just because of the way he looked – and the type to answer back when stopped and questioned, as he occasionally was, coming home in the small hours from some club.

'Anyway, are you all right?' Nick continued.

'More frightened than hurt. Just a few cuts and bruises.'

'What happened?'

'Brake-cables went and I came off, that's all.' Kate decided to change the subject. 'What's all this about packing in college?'

'I decided I'd had enough. Exams were a disaster and I don't give a monkeys about Politics, Philosophy or Economics anyway!'

'Why don't you change courses?'

'What's the point, it's all the same old academic rubbish.'

36

'So what are you going to do?'

Nick gave the careless grin that drove his father mad. 'Dunno! Something will turn up.'

'Like a park bench and a can of Special Brew?'

'Sounds good to me.'

Kate thumped him in the ribs, and ducked the mock clout he aimed at her head. It was never any use arguing with Nick, it just made him worse. If his father left him alone he'd probably see sense. Unfortunately there wasn't much chance of that.

'Maybe you'd better not come back with me,' said Kate as they reached the corner of her street. 'Maggie's been hassling Dad and he's on the warpath.'

'Doesn't bother me,' said Nick carelessly. 'I'm not scared of him. I promised Maggie I'd talk to him, might as well get it over with.'

Kate sighed. 'All right, but for goodness sake don't argue. Shut up and listen to whatever he tells you and promise you'll think about it.'

'Whose side are you on, anyway?'

'Nobody's. You can do what you like, I just don't want any more rows.'

Nick put on his angelic expression. 'Me, row? How is life in Carter Towers anyway?'

'A lot quieter since you left.'

'Quiet as the grave I should think. I don't know how you stand it. How's Lady Penelope and the Infant Prodigy?'

Nick still seemed to resent the way Susan and

37

Chrissie had replaced him and Maggie – even though he and his mother had both left of their own accord.

'They're all right,' said Kate.

'And Jiminy Cricket?'

'Same as ever,' said Kate.

Jon and Nick had never really got on. Jon frequently disapproved of Nick's behaviour and never failed to let him know it, even from an early age. Nick started calling him 'Jiminy Cricket' after Pinocchio's conscience in the old Disney film.

'It's bad enough being criticised all the time by Dad,' Nick used to say. 'Being ticked off by your baby brother as well is just too much!'

Susan was stirring a big pan of spaghetti as they came into the kitchen and Chrissie was laying the table.

Susan gave Nick a welcoming smile. 'Lunch is nearly ready, Nick. Your father's just gone down to the off-licence. Stay and eat.' Susan was a bit wary of Nick, but she tried to stay on good terms with him.

'Thanks, I'd love to,' said Nick. Even though he made fun of Susan behind her back, he was always polite enough to her face.

Jack came into the kitchen with a bottle of wine. He looked at Nick and grunted. 'Trust you to turn up in time for a free meal!'

'Susan invited me,' said Nick. 'I hope it's not too much strain on the budget.' It was a bad start, and it soon got worse.

Jon came down from his room and slid into

his chair. He muttered a hello to Nick, and refused even to look at Kate.

Susan shared out spaghetti and bolognese sauce and the meal got under way.

It wasn't long before the subject of Nick leaving college came up. In no time at all, the discussion turned into a first class row. Jack's temper rose higher as the level in the wine bottle sank. Kate tucked into her spaghetti bolognese, letting the storm rage over her. Quite like old times, she thought. Well, let 'em get on with it.

Pretty soon the row rose to its inevitable climax.

'Your trouble is you don't care about anything,' shouted Jack, his face red with rage. 'Not about me, your mother, or even yourself.'

'I care about being left alone to lead my own life,' yelled Nick. 'I left here so as not to have to listen to you shouting the odds, and I'm dammed if I know why I came back for more.' He rose and nodded to Susan. 'Thanks for the meal.'

Jack Carter lolled back in his chair. 'Aren't you forgetting something?'

'Like what?'

'You've forgotten to cadge a few quid off me. That's usually why you come, isn't it?' He fished a crumpled fiver from his back pocket, screwed it up and tossed it contemptuously across the table at Nick. 'I'm afraid this is all I can spare. When it runs out you'll just have to stand on the corner and ask people for their spare change. Might as well get started on your new career!'

Nick took the bank-note, squeezed it into an

even tighter ball and hurled the wadded-up fiver straight into his father's face. With a roar of rage Jack Carter jumped to his feet, his chair crashing over behind him. 'I never gave you a good hiding when you were a kid Nick, but it's not too late!'

'Oh yes it is,' said Nick, who was even bigger than his father now. 'Don't try it, or you might get more than you bargain for. All I need is the excuse.'

Time seemed to stop for a moment as the two men confronted each other. Kate thought how alike they were despite the difference in years. The same square jaws, wide shoulders, angry black eyes, big hands clenched into massive fists.

Jon and Susan sat white-faced and silent, too terrified to speak. Kate saw Chrissie looking fascinatedly from Jack to Nick, her huge dark eyes seeming to swallow them both up.

'Nick!' shouted Kate. 'Pack it in!'

Nick looked at her for a moment, shrugged helplessly, and then turned and marched out of the room. Jack kicked aside his chair and rushed out after him.

Susan looked worriedly at Kate. 'Shouldn't we do something?'

Kate shook her head disgustedly. 'Stupid twits. Leave them to it! I don't suppose they'll do each other any harm.'

As if to contradict her, a shattering crash came from the front door, mingled with a yell of fear and pain. Kate jumped up and sprinted down the short hallway.

Her father was standing just outside the front

doorway, at the top of the steps. He was leaning against the left-hand pedestal for support, his face white with shock. The pedestal rocked a little and Kate realised that the huge concrete flower pot was missing.

Nick lay on the pavement at the bottom of the steps, his face as white as his father's, surrounded by the shattered fragments of the pot. He was clutching his shoulder and bleeding from a cut on his forehead.

The two men seemed frozen in a strange tableau. There was a haze of concrete dust in the air. It settled on their clothes in a fine white powder. The only sound was the hoarse rasping of Jack's breathing.

Kate ran down the steps. 'Nick, what happened?'

Nick struggled to a sitting position and looked up. 'He tried to kill me! Chucked that ruddy great pot at me!'

Jack shook his head as if to clear it. 'No,' he said thickly. 'It was an accident.'

'Accident?' shouted Nick in a shaking voice. 'Some accident! I'd just got to the bottom of the steps when that thing whizzed by me. It was so close it grazed my shoulder. A few inches higher and it would've cracked my skull! It knocked me flying and smashed on the ground there.'

Kate helped him to get up. 'Are you sure you're all right? You must have been cut by a bit of flying concrete. Come inside and get cleaned up.'

Nick got to his feet and backed away. 'Forget

it, you're not getting me back in there with that lunatic. He tried to kill me, I tell you!'

Shrugging off Kate's hand, Nick turned and disappeared down the street in a shambling run.

Kate went up the steps to her father. 'Dad, what happened?'

Jack looked dazedly at her. 'I'm not sure. I ran out here after Nick . . . I remember I tripped and fell forwards . . . I put out my hand to grab the pot and it just . . . flew off the pedestal, straight towards Nick.' He looked at Kate his eyes wide with horror. 'I never wanted to hurt Nick, I wouldn't do that. It was an accident I tell you, a freak accident.'

By now Susan and Chrissie and Jon had come out onto the doorstep. At Jack's words, Kate glanced instinctively at Jon, and at the bike shed.

Another freak accident. The first nearly killed her, the second nearly killed Nick. Two near-deaths in two days. It just had to be more than coincidence.

Kate felt frightened and helpless. They were being stalked by an unknown enemy, and she felt certain of just one thing. The nightmare wasn't over yet. The enemy was going to strike again.

Next time somebody might die.

FIVE

Suddenly Kate realised that Jack was stumbling down the steps. 'Nick,' he called. 'Come back!'

He started to follow after Nick, but Kate ran after him and grabbed his arm.

'Better let him go, Dad. He's not really hurt but he's pretty shaken up. You don't look too well yourself.'

Her father shook his head dazedly. 'You don't understand, Kate; Nick thinks I tried to kill him. I'd never do that. I've got to explain, make him see . . .'

'Later, Dad,' said Kate firmly. She led him back up the steps and handed him over to Susan who had appeared in the doorway.

'Make him some nice strong tea and get him to sit down for a bit. We'll sort things out when everyone's calmed down.'

Jack and Susan went inside and Kate stood surveying the mess. There were bits of masonry scattered all the way down the front steps, with most of the debris piled up at the bottom.

By now Mrs Pearson their next-door neighbour was on her doorstep, eyes gleaming with curiosity and malice. She always took a keen interest in the Carters and their affairs – so she could give the rest of the neighbours the inside story. Come to that, curtains were probably twitching all down the street. Well, to hell with them, thought Kate.

'Had an accident, dear?' asked Mrs Pearson.

Kate waved at the wreckage on the steps. 'The pot fell off the pedestal, just missed my brother Nick as he was going down the steps. It gave him a bit of a fright.'

'It's lucky no one was hurt.'

Someone will be if you don't shut up, thought Kate. I'll crown you with the other pot! Out loud, she just said, 'Yes, isn't it?'

Turning away from her nosy neighbour, Kate went down the steps, through the side-gate and along the little passage that led to the garden. She got a stiff broom, a shovel and a green garden rubbish bag from the shed, and started cleaning up the mess. She was still thinking about the accident. How had it happened? How *could* it have happened?

As if in answer to her thoughts a voice said, 'Could have been the frost.'

It was Jon. He came down the front steps and started picking up chunks of masonry and putting them in the sack.

Kate looked cautiously at him, then went on sweeping the steps. 'What do you mean, frost?'

'Water gets in the cracks in the concrete. When it freezes in winter it turns into ice.'

'So?'

'So it expands – the volume of the ice is bigger than the water,' explained Jon impatiently. 'That's why you get burst pipes.' He looked up at the remaining urn. 'If the cement had cracked, that first urn could have been just balanced there. So when Dad leaned against it . . .' He paused. 'All the same – there's something funny about the accident.'

'What do you mean, funny?'

Jon pointed to the remaining pot. 'Look how big those things are. Even if Dad did knock one off accidentally, it would just have dropped straight down, not flown through the air. The broken bits would have been at the top of the steps, not the bottom.'

Kate stared at him. 'But it *did* fly through the air. Nick said it just missed him – it bruised his shoulder. And he was down at the bottom of the steps, right on the pavement.'

'That's right,' agreed Jon. 'And most of the mess is at the bottom of the steps as well.'

A unpleasant thought came into Kate's mind. 'So you're saying Dad must have grabbed the flowerpot and chucked it at Nick after all – just as Nick said.'

'Looks like it. But . . .'

'But what?'

'Those pots must weigh a ton. Dad's a big bloke but I doubt if he *could* have chucked it that far.'

'Let's try an experiment,' said Kate suddenly. 'We'll shove the other pot off, see how far we can throw it!'

'Kate!'

Just as when she'd suggested some mischievous scheme when they were both younger, the straight-laced Jon was horrified. And just as she always had in those days, Kate over-rode his objections, carrying him along with her plan.

'Come on!' Kate ran up the steps and started shoving at the right-hand pot. It moved – not far, but it definitely moved.

'It's loose all right,' shouted Kate. 'Come on, help me!'

With Jon's reluctant help, Kate found she could move the pot quite easily. The cement that was supposed to be holding it in place had simply crumbled away over the years.

They rocked the pot to and fro between them, until it was clear that it was free-standing on the pedestal.

'Right,' said Kate. 'Now, come round behind it with me and we'll grab the pot between us and throw it as far as we can.'

'Kate, I really don't think we should . . .'

'Rubbish!' said Kate. 'Come on!'

Reluctantly, Jon took his place at her side and they both grabbed the pot.

'On the count of three,' ordered Kate. 'One – two – three – throw!'

They threw – or rather they tried. The big stone pot just toppled slowly from the pedestal and crashed at its foot, breaking into several big pieces.

'See?' said Jon.

Kate saw. The bits of broken urn were just

where Jon said they would be – right at the foot of the pillar. They hadn't thrown it any distance at all.

Jack came rushing out of the front door. 'What the hell's going on now?'

'Just getting rid of the other urn for you,' said Kate.

'You mean you smashed that thing on purpose?'

'No point in having just one, is there? Makes the whole place look lopsided.'

'You're mad,' said her father furiously. 'Sometimes I think this whole family's mad. Just clear up that mess!'

Kate and Jon went on clearing up the mess – there was twice as much of it now. Kate looked thoughtfully at Jon as he sorted out the mess in his usual methodical way, big chunks of concrete in the sack first, smaller ones gathered into a tidy pile. Good old Jon, neat and tidy as ever. Her mind went back to the bike accident. Surely Jon wouldn't really have tried to hurt her? But she had caught him coming out of the garden shed looking guilty, and he'd been waiting on the steps to see the results.

Suddenly Kate couldn't stand the suspense any longer. She swung round on Jon. 'Last night when I came off my bike, I saw you coming out of the garden shed just before, right?'

Jon nodded, but he didn't speak.

'You'd done something to my bike hadn't you?'

He nodded again. 'I thought you knew. Isn't

that why you've been giving me the cold shoulder ever since?'

'What do you expect? You nearly killed me!'

'Just by giving you a couple of flat tyres?'

'Just by what?'

'I got a long needle and put a tiny hole in each innertube, front and back. I thought the tyres would go down by the time you got to the end of the street and you'd have to push the bike back up again. That's why I was waiting for you, so I could have a good laugh. I didn't know you'd come off the bike.'

'Both tyres *were* flat,' said Kate slowly. 'Jason said so in the bike shop the next day, it just didn't sink in.'

'I know it was a stupid thing to do – I don't know what got into me. I was mad about my room, and about my sore nose. It's humiliating being beaten up by your sister. I just wanted to give you a hard time, I didn't dream your brakes would go too and there'd be an accident. I tried to say I was sorry last night but you wouldn't talk to me.'

'That's all you did – puncture the tyres?'

'Yes, of course. Why?'

'You didn't touch the brakes?'

'Of course not,' said Jon indignantly. 'I was angry but I wasn't trying to kill you! Do you think I'm mad?'

Kate's mind felt like a kaleidoscope, whirling with a dozen different thoughts and feelings. 'I'm not sure what I think . . .'

Jon gave her a frightened look. 'What's going

on Kate? First the bike, then this. Everything's suddenly gone crazy!'

'I know,' said Kate. 'I know. Ever since Friday . . .'

They finished clearing up, bagged the rubbish and went back into the house. Jon went up to his room and Kate went to look for the others. She found Susan and her father drinking coffee in the kitchen. Apparently Chrissie was upstairs in bed.

'The thing is, all these upsets are so bad for her,' Susan was saying. 'She's been on edge since yesterday and now this.'

Kate poured herself some coffee. 'The mess is all tidied up,' she said. 'Is Chrissie not well, Susan?'

'She's a bit upset. The school says she needs a calm peaceful atmosphere and . . .' Susan shrugged helplessly.

'And this isn't it,' said Kate. 'I'm sorry Susan, we're not usually this bad.'

Jack said, 'I shall have to find Nick somehow and make up with him. Quite apart from anything else, I'll get an earbashing from Maggie if I don't.'

'I'd leave it for a while,' said Kate. 'Nick needs time to calm down.'

Later that evening Kate sat on her bed, her mind a whirl of speculation. She remembered her conversation with Jason in the bike shop, when she'd told him about her accident.

'Both brake-cables went when I was going down the hill.'

'Both of 'em?'

'Both. At exactly the same time. What d'you reckon the chances of that are?'

'About a million to one. Must have been a real freak accident.'

'If it was an accident.'

She remembered Jon's anguished face as he'd confessed to puncturing her tyres. That story was totally believable, just the sort of silly trick Jon would play. But trying to murder her . . .

And now there'd been another impossible accident. Surely Jon couldn't have caused that one? How could he have known that Dad would stumble out and dislodge the pedestal? Maybe the trap had really been meant for her all along, thought Kate wildly. Perhaps Jon had planned to follow her next time she was leaving the house and give the big flowerpot a shove . . .

But then, the second accident had been as impossible as the first. How could the massive pot have flown through the air, just missing Nick's head? Their experiment had proved that there was no way that Jack could have chucked the massive stone pot so far. The idea of Jon trying to throw it was even more ridiculous. Anyway, it was Jon who'd pointed out that the pot was too big to throw. Or was that just a bluff, to confuse her?

Kate shook her head, trying to get her thoughts into some kind of logical order.

Her first suspicions had been bad enough. It was terrible to think that her brother might have tried to kill her, or that her father had tried to harm Nick. But Kate was beginning to realise that the only other explanation was even more terrifying.

If Jon and her father didn't cause either of those accidents, someone else did. Kate shivered. That someone – or something – must have some very strange and evil powers. And it must hate the Carter family. It had tried to kill her, putting the blame on Jon. It had tried to kill Nick, putting the blame on her father.

So who was next?

SIX

Nick sat at the bar in the Castle, poshest pub in town, nursing his pint and glaring resentfully at all the prosperous looking people around him.

They were all happy, laughing, having a good time. *They* had glamorous girlfriends, plenty of cash. *They* probably had decent dads who didn't try to clobber them with stone flowerpots. It just wasn't fair.

A fresh surge of rage went through Nick at the memory of the quarrel with his father. It was odd really. Although his temper, like his father's, was short, it was usually short-lived as well. But this particular row seemed to be living on inside him, seething and boiling, a raging storm in his blood that refused to die down.

Draining his glass, Nick fished a handful of coins from his pocket and counted them. Just enough for one more pint. He slammed the money down on the counter and growled, 'Pinterlager!'

Like all good landlords, the man behind the bar kept a careful eye on his customers. This big, scruffy young man with the cut face, scowling into his beer and muttering, looked like bad news.

He said, 'Sorry mate!'

Nick looked up. 'Come again?'

'You've had enough. Better be on your way.'

With a growing sense of outrage Nick realised that the man thought he was drunk. The unfairness of it! He wasn't drunk, he couldn't afford to be. He only had enough cash for two pints and he hadn't even had the second one yet.

'Look, I want another drink!'

'Not in here.'

The middle-aged landlord was a hefty type, a bit overweight. He's putting you down, just like your father, said a voice inside Nick's head. Go on, hit him, he deserves it!

Nick had a sudden violent impulse to hurl his stool at the man behind the bar. But there were other barmen nearby, and a massive type who looked very like a bouncer was edging closer.

Snatching up his money Nick shouldered his way through the crowd and went outside the pub.

It was unfortunate that the plump young man drew up at just that moment. He was driving a flashy sports car, and he wore designer slacks, an expensive blazer and a silk shirt. He was sleek-haired, and he seemed to float in a cloud of expensive aftershave. His round pink face had an expression of conscious superiority. He even had a long-legged, long-haired blonde in the passenger seat of the car.

He was everything Nick loathed.

The young man jumped out of the sports car and found Nick standing directly in his way. 'Do you mind?' he said wearily.

'Look at him,' said the voice in Nick's head. 'He's got everything and you've got nothing. He despises you. Smash him!'

When Nick didn't move, the young man said, 'Oh all right . . . Though I must say you look big and strong enough to work. Here!' He handed Nick a fifty pence coin.

Nick heard another voice inside his head – the sneering tones of his father: *'You can stand on the corner and ask people for their spare change. Might as well get started on your new career!'*

Nick grabbed the plump young man by his belt and by his collar and swung him high above his head, like a weight-lifter with a barbell. It was all quite effortless – the young man might have been an inflatable dummy. Nick held him up in the air for a moment, wondering what to do next. Chuck him through the window of the pub and take the car and the girl for a nice long drive? She looked like the sympathetic type, he could tell her all his troubles – as soon as she stopped screaming . . .

Unfortunately – or perhaps fortunately, all things considered – two patrolling policemen chose this moment to come round the corner of the pub.

Jack slammed down the phone. 'Still not there. That must be about the fiftieth time I've tried to call him.'

'Then he's not in, is he?' said Kate practically. 'If I know Nick he's out drowning his sorrows somewhere.'

54

'Maybe I ought to go out and look for him.'

'In every pub in town? Who would we send to look for you?' They were in the sitting room. Susan was upstairs with Chrissie, Jon had disappeared into his room, and Kate was getting fed up with watching her father trying to phone Nick. It was interesting to see how much he really cared about Nick, despite their constant quarrels.

Jack paced moodily up and down the room. 'All the same, Kate . . .'

'Look, Dad, this isn't the first fight you've had with Nick. This time tomorrow he'll be as sorry as you are.'

'It's the first fight that ended up with me trying to murder him – at least, that's what Nick thinks.'

Kate fell silent. The business with the flowerpot did make a difference.

Her father looked out of the sitting room window as a smart saloon car drew up near the house.

'Oh my God!'

'What is it?'

'It's your mother. That's all I need.'

Kate joined him at the window. They watched Maggie get out of her car and march towards the house. As always she looked neat, smart and determined.

'Now we're for it,' muttered Jack. 'I know that look.'

The doorbell jangled fiercely. 'Well,' said Kate. 'Are you going to let her in? Or shall we hide behind the sofa until she goes away?'

Her father gave her a harried look. 'You go, Kate.'

Kate went to the front door and opened it. 'Hello, Mum.'

Ignoring the greeting Maggie said, 'Where's your father?'

'Front room. Come – '

Maggie brushed past her and strode down the hall. Kate followed. 'Do come in,' she muttered. 'Lovely to see you, too!'

When she reached the front room her parents were already confronting each other.

Jack Carter was leaning on the mantelpiece doing his best to look casual. Maggie stood in the doorway, poised to attack.

Just like the beginning of a boxing-match, thought Kate.

Maggie threw the first punch. 'I've been trying to ring you for ages.'

'Phone's been tied up,' grunted Jack. 'I've been trying to call Nick. He came round at lunchtime and well, we had a bit of a dust-up. I've been trying to get hold of him to sort things out. Trouble is, he's not in, and I've no idea where he is.'

'I can tell you where he is,' said Maggie icily. 'In prison.'

There was a shocked silence.

Kate remembered her mother's habit of dramatic exaggeration. 'Oh no he isn't,' she said. 'Not in the few hours since lunchtime – unless English justice has speeded up considerably. I suppose you mean he's down the local nick?'

'Is that all it means to you?' said Maggie. 'Your own brother a common criminal, in danger of prison . . .'

'Knock it off, Mum,' said Kate wearily. 'Whatever's happened to Nick is quite bad enough without you turning it into some stupid melodrama.'

Maggie swung round on her, her hand raised. Although their father had never hit them when they were little, Maggie had handed our frequent clips on the ear.

Not any more though, thought Kate. She found herself taking a step forward. 'Just try it!'

Jack shouted, 'Pack it in, you two! What's the matter with everyone? Just tell us what's happened, will you, Maggie? And for goodness sake sit down!'

'I got a call from Nick at the police station about half an hour ago,' said Maggie. 'He sounded – strange.'

'Drunk?' asked Jack bluntly.

'Not really. More – confused. As if he didn't really know what was going on. He said he'd been charged with, oh, I don't know, "common assault", something ridiculous. I tried to call you but the phone was always busy.'

'You didn't think of going down to the police station yourself?' asked Kate.

Maggie looked oddly at her. 'Naturally I thought your father ought to know.'

'Quite right,' said Jack, taking charge as usual. 'I'll see if I can get hold of Charlie Salter.' He looked at his watch. 'He'll be playing golf, but

he ought to be back in the clubhouse by now.'
Charlie Salter was the firm's solicitor.

Jack grabbed the phone and dialled. 'Hello? Is
Mr Salter still in the clubhouse? Put him on will
you . . . Jack Carter. Tell him it's an emergency
. . . Hello, Charlie? Sorry to bother you, something's come up . . .'

As Jack explained what had happened, Maggie
and Kate were left eyeing one another cautiously.

Finally Maggie said, 'How are things, Kate?'

'Things have been a bit weird.'

'Weird? How exactly?'

'Someone wrecked Jon's room; Jon and I had
a fight; I had an accident on my bike; Nick came
round and had a row with dad; there was an
accident with a stone urn . . . And now this! I'm
begging to think fate's got it in for this family.
It's "The Curse of the Carters."'

Maggie shivered and Kate remembered how
superstitious she was.

'You shouldn't say such things, Kate. Talking about bad things makes them happen. And
how's . . .'

'Susan,' said Kate irritably. 'Her name's Susan,
Mum.'

Maggie always made a pretence of being unable
to remember her ex-husband's new wife's name.
Even though she'd walked out on her husband,
she was quite capable of resenting anyone else
who walked in.

A quiet voice said, 'Hello Maggie, how are
you?'

Susan had appeared in the doorway. For a

moment the two women looked at each other with all the wariness of two strange cats.

Jack slammed down the phone. 'Charlie will meet us at the station.' He put an arm around Susan. 'Have they told you what's happened? Nick's got himself arrested; Maggie came round to tell me. I'm afraid I'll have to go down the station.'

'Yes, I'm sure you will,' said Susan quietly.

Kate gave her a quick look, then turned to her parents. 'I'll come too. You two need a referee!'

They drove to the police station in Maggie's car. It was a flash-looking Mazda saloon, newer and more expensive than Jack's battered old Volvo. Kate sat in the back, her father in the front passenger seat beside Maggie. There wasn't much conversation on the way. Now and again Kate saw her father wince at Maggie's carefree driving style, but he managed not to say anything.

It had been one of the many causes of dispute before the divorce, Kate remembered. Maggie drove with what she liked to call flair. Jack called it sheer bloody carelessness.

Kate couldn't remember how many times Maggie had come home with dented bumpers or side-panels and a convincing story about how it had all been the other driver's fault.

'The man was a perfect fool, I tell you. I signalled perfectly clearly. I really don't know why they allow some of these people on the roads!'

That was one of Maggie's great strengths,

thought Kate. She was always absolutely sure that any problems were someone else's fault. Like now, for instance. Nick was in trouble because Jack wasn't carrying out his duties as a father.

Though in this case, there was probably something in it. Kate was pretty sure that the row with Jack had sent Nick away in a mood to look for trouble. Apparently he'd found it.

They parked in the tree-lined square behind the police station. It was just getting dark and black shadows were gathering between the trees. Kate felt there was something sinister about this shadowy little square. It was the way the tall houses and the trees seemed to crowd in on you. Someone had been mugged there recently. A young woman – she'd been half-strangled apparently. There'd been a lot of fuss about such a violent crime taking place right behind the police station.

They went round to the front steps of the station and found Charlie Salter, Jack's solicitor, waiting for them. He was a stocky grey-haired man with heavy horn-rimmed glasses. Usually he was cheerful and jokey, but he looked grim and serious now. Kate supposed it was his legal face.

Jack said, 'Thanks, Charlie. Sorry to drag you out at the weekend.'

Maggie rushed to him and said, 'Charlie, thank goodness you're here! Can you do anything to help Nick?'

Charlie Salter was a family friend and he knew

Maggie of old. He'd even handled the divorce. He looked at Maggie over his glasses and said, 'Very likely.'

He nodded to Kate and they all went inside.

It was waiting after that, endless waitng.

There were discussions with the station sergeant, who was middle-aged and fatherly, and with the station inspector who looked surprisingly young and extremely severe.

Kate wasn't allowed to take part so she just hung around on the fringes of things. Jack, Maggie and Charlie Salter were shown into a bare interview room. Kate caught a glimpse of Nick, looking very young and scared, then the door closed behind them.

More waiting. Kate sat in the little reception area and a policewoman brought her a cup of tea. No one came in, no one came out. It was obviously a quiet night at the nick. Kate finished her tea. After a while her head started to nod . . .

Time was dragging at the Carter house, too. Chrissie had insisted on staying up. It was long past her bedtime, but she was wide awake. She was tearful and fretful, and nothing her mother did seemed to settle her.

Jon was restless as well. He'd been unsettled ever since Susan told him what had happened, wandering aimlessly about the house.

Susan looked up as he came into the sitting room. 'Still no news, I'm afraid.'

'You could ring them.'

'I did. Some sergeant said, "Matters were still under discussion" – whatever that means.'

Chrissie whimpered, her head in her mother's lap. Susan stroked her hair.

'What's the matter with her?' asked Jon wearily.

'Something seems to have upset her. It's no good trying to get her to go to sleep when she's like this.'

'Why don't we all go down there?' said Jon suddenly. 'You could take us in Dad's car. Better than hanging around here. Chrissie would like a car ride, wouldn't you Chrissie?'

Chrissie raised her head from her mother's lap and stared at him.

A door slammed and Kate woke up with a start. Maggie was standing over her.

Kate yawned. 'Any news?'

'Just endless legal wrangling. And now I've run out of cigarettes.'

Kate didn't approve of smoking. As far as she was concerned, Maggie's fagless state was her own problem.

'Tough,' said Kate. 'Tell you what, this'd be a good chance for you to give up. You're always saying you're going to one day.'

Maggie gave her a murderous look. 'I think I've got some cigarettes in the car. Otherwise, I'll have to go and buy some.'

She looked at Kate expectantly.

'See you later then,' said Kate.

Maggie marched angrily away. They'd kept

her hanging around this ghastly little police station for ages, and now Kate wouldn't do the simplest thing for her.

Underneath Maggie's anger was a very real concern for Nick. For all her sophisticated manner, she had an almost childlike fear of authority, and she found the atmosphere of the police station terrifying. She made her way round the back and headed across the shadowed square towards her car.

It was dark now, especially under the trees where the car was parked. She peered into the blackness. It seemed to move somehow. Was there someone there? Telling herself she was being silly, Maggie walked into the shadows – and suddenly the darkness became solid. A black shape rose up before her, smothered her, and bore her suffocating to the ground.

SEVEN

Minutes after Maggie's departure, Kate heard another door slamming and the sound of voices. She looked up and saw a little group coming down the corridor towards her. There was her father, Charlie Salter, and to her astonishment, Nick.

Kate jumped up excitedly. 'Nick!'

Her father gave her a broad grin. 'Coming, Kate?'

She looked at her brother. 'Nick too? They're letting him go?'

'Released with an official caution,' said Charlie Salter. 'The victim was too embarrassed to make any charges. Dead lucky to get off so lightly, if I say so myself.'

'Thanks to you, Charlie,' said Jack.

'And you,' said Nick, grinning affectionately at his father. 'The way you stood up for me, it sounded like I was little Lord Fauntleroy making my first minor slip!'

'You deserve ten years on a chain gang at the very least,' said Kate. 'No wonder society's in such a state!'

She gave Nick a rib-cracking hug.

'Right,' said Jack. 'Let's get out of here before they come to their senses and change their minds!'

'I'll say goodbye,' said Charlie Salter. 'I'll be sending you a bill, Jack!' Waving away their thanks he disappeared into the night.

Nick looked round. 'Where's Maggie?'

He sounded disappointed and Kate said quickly, 'She had to go back to the car for something. Let's go and tell her the good news. Come on, you lot!'

She ran out of the police station and turned down the little side alley. When she emerged into the square Maggie was nowhere to be seen. 'Maybe she's having a quiet cigarette in the car,' thought Kate. She hurried across the square towards Maggie's car. Peering through the shadows she caught a glimpse of a dark billowing shape on the ground.

'Maggie,' she called. 'Maggie, where are you?'

The dark shape seemed to shimmer and disappear – leaving behind it the crumpled figure of Maggie.

Kate ran and knelt beside her. 'Maggie, are you all right? What happened?'

Maggie clutched Kate's arm. She was still conscious but gasping for air. 'This horrible black shape . . . attacked me . . . it was suffocating me . . . I couldn't call out, couldn't even breathe . . .'

Kate helped her to her feet. Maggie was shaking with fear, but she didn't seem to be hurt.

Footsteps pounded across the square. It was Nick, with Jack close behind him.

'What's happened?' called Nick.

'I'm not sure. Maggie's been attacked.'

Nick put an arm round his mother's shoulder. She was still shaking with fear. 'What was it, Mum, a mugger?'

'Not just robbery . . .' she gasped. 'Tried to kill me . . .'

'It's all right,' said Nick. 'Whoever it was has gone.'

Puffing a little, Jack came hurrying up. 'What happened, Kate? Did you see anything?'

'Not really, just a dark shape. It vanished when I ran up.'

'We'd better check the square, Nick,' said Jack. 'The beggar may still be hiding somewhere.'

'I just hope he is . . .'

The two men moved away.

'Where are they going?' cried Maggie hysterically.

'Just checking everything's safe,' said Kate soothingly. 'Do you want to sit in the car?'

Maggie nodded, turned and gave a piercing scream. A dark hooded shape had appeared from between the cars.

For a moment Kate was scared as well. Then she saw it was Susan in the old-fashioned hooded cape she sometimes wore.

'Susan! What are you doing here?'

'We got tired of waiting and came to see what was going on. The others are in the car. What's the matter with Maggie?'

Maggie's scream had brought Nick and his father running back across the square. They arrived just as Maggie pointed a shaking finger at Susan.

'It was you – you attacked me!'

Susan didn't reply. She stood there, looking quietly at her accuser.

'You've always hated me,' screamed Maggie. 'You tried to kill me!'

'Stop it, Maggie,' shouted Jack. 'You're hysterical, you're talking rubbish. Susan doesn't want to hurt you. She's not big enough to do you much harm if she did.'

'Haven't you ever heard of the strength of madness?' sobbed Maggie. 'She's mad, Jack, her and that creepy kid of hers. Get rid of her before she kills us all!'

'Stop it!' shouted Jack. He grabbed her shoulders and shook her. Maggie collapsed into incoherent sobs.

Nick swung round angrily and grabbed the front of his father's coat. 'What the hell do you think you're doing?'

Jack wrenched himself free and the two men glared at each other. Kate could feel the violence in the air.

She raised her voice. 'What's the matter with you all? Have you all gone mad? Calm down everyone!'

There was a stunned silence as if everyone was suddenly shocked by the strength of their own emotions. Jack shook his head. 'We're all a bit upset. Sorry, Maggie, sorry Nick.'

Kate turned to Nick. 'Take Mum back to her flat and stay with her till she's okay, will you? I don't think she'll want to come home with us. We'll meet up tomorrow.'

Nick nodded and helped Maggie into the car.

Jack Carter rubbed his hands across his eyes. He turned and looked down at Susan. 'How did you get here?'

'We got tired of waiting for news at home, so Jon suggested we all came down here to the police station.'

'Where are the kids?'

'Chrissie got scared at the idea of going into a police station, so Jon said he'd stay with her in the car. We're parked over the other side of the square. I went round to the station but they said you'd all just gone so I came back here.'

They walked across to the other side of the square where Jack's old Volvo was parked. Chrissie was asleep in the back seat, but there was no sign of Jon.

'Dad, look!' whispered Kate.

Not far away a dark shape had appeared between the trees. Jack swung round, fists raised.

'It's only me,' called a familiar voice.

It was Jon in his baggy black sweater, the one that had caused all the trouble.

'This square's full of sinister shapes in black tonight,' thought Kate. 'It's like a vampire's convention.'

'You were supposed to be looking after Chrissie,' said Susan.

Jon shrugged. 'She fell asleep. I didn't feel like sitting in the car so I went for a wander around.

It's all right, I was never out of sight of the car. What's happening about Nick? And what was all that fuss over there?'

'Maggie was attacked,' said Jack.

'Who by?'

'We don't know,' said Kate. 'I got a quick glimpse of someone in black.'

Jon seemed genuinely astonished by the news. 'Is she hurt? Where is she?'

'Nick's driving her home. She's badly shaken but she's all right.

Jon looked baffled. 'I thought Nick had been arrested?'

'He got off with a caution,' said Kate. 'I'll explain when we get back. For goodness sake let's go home.'

Jack and Susan got in the front and Jon and Kate got in the back with Chrissie, one each side of her. She muttered and stirred when they got in, but was too drowsy to sit up.

Jack started the car and they set off for home.

'So what happened to Maggie?' asked Jon.

'She says she was attacked, knocked to the ground,' said Jack wearily. 'Did it really happen Kate, or did she trip up and imagine it all?'

'There was something there all right,' said Kate. 'It was all shadow and all in black, so I didn't really see anything much at all.'

'Might have been a mugger, I suppose,' said Jack. 'Some kid after her handbag, or the keys to the car.'

'Maggie said it tried to suffocate her,' said Kate.

Jon said, 'Why didn't you go to the police then?'

There was an awkward silence. No one wanted to mention Maggie's wild accusation.

Jack said, 'Well, she wasn't hurt, no real harm done. And I think we'd had enough of police stations by then.'

'Not to mention the fact that she accused me of being the one who attacked her,' said Susan in a quietly furious voice. 'That might have been a bit embarrassing, two Carters arrested in one day. Though I suppose I'm not really a proper Carter, just an imitation.'

Kate felt Chrissie go rigid beside her at the sound of her mother's angry voice.

'She was hysterical,' said Jack. 'Maggie will say anything when she's like that.'

'You never know, she might be right,' said Susan. 'Maybe I did try to kill her.'

There was a note of hysteria in her voice, and Jack Carter glanced at her uneasily. 'That's just Maggie's crazy talk, love. You could never harm anyone.'

'I didn't notice you defending me to Maggie. Me or my creepy kid. Maybe I am crazy! Maybe I want to kill you all!'

Suddenly Susan grabbed the wheel and wrenched it hard, sending the car heading for the side of the road.

Jack stamped on the brake in an emergency stop and the car screeched to a halt, inches from a massive plane tree.

'Hell and damnation!' said Jack.

The jolt frightened Chrisse and she started crying. Kate tried to soothe her.

'What the hell do you think you're doing?' yelled Jack. 'You nearly did kill us then! Has everyone in this family gone raving mad?'

It's the first time he's ever yelled at her, thought Kate.

Susan looked at her husband with tear-filled eyes. 'Jack, I'm sorry, I don't know what got into me . . .'

Jack drew a deep breath. 'All right. But for heaven's sake don't you go hysterical on me.'

'It's a Carter madness,' said Jon. 'Like "folie à deux!"'

Kate turned round and glared at him. 'What are you on about now?'

'"Folie à deux" means madness for two,' said Jon.

'I do know a bit of basic French,' said Kate. 'What about it?'

'It's when you get two people who are quite normal by themselves but go crazy if you put them together. Like us Carters. We're all right apart, but together we drive each other crazy. Now Susan's got it too – proves she's a real Carter.'

Chrissie was still crying despite all Kate's attempts to calm her.

'I think I'd better go in the back,' said Susan. 'Will you change places Kate?'

They changed seats and Kate looked across at her father. 'Well, if the excitement's over, can we please go home?'

For Kate Carter it was to be another restless night.

They had a quiet enough evening when they got home, a light supper, a bit of telly and early nights all round. Jon disappeared as usual, whether to go to bed or stay up all night with his computer nobody knew.

It wouldn't have surprised Kate if he turned into a bat and fluttered off into the night. She felt nothing could surprise her now.

The kaleidoscope had shifted once again, but the new pattern was even more puzzling and sinister than the old one. There were new shapes in the pattern now.

That extraordinary business with the flower-pot. Had her father really chucked it at Nick? Maybe he'd been brooding over Nick's behaviour for some time, resenting his rudeness and the way he always sided with Maggie. Perhaps he really had thrown the pot, with all the savage strength of a murderous rage. Kate shuddered at the thought. If the pot had hit him, it would have smashed Nick's skull like an eggshell.

And Nick himself. She still hadn't got the full story of why he'd been arrested – there'd been no time last night – but apparently he'd attacked some perfect stranger for no reason at all. What had got into him? Nick was no angel but he'd never been in such bad trouble before – and he'd certainly never harmed anybody.

And what about Maggie? That performance in the square had been over the top, even for her. Did she really think Susan had attacked her? Was she simply over-dramatising as usual? Did she just want to make trouble between Jack and Susan?

She'd certainly managed to do that. Susan's outburst in the car had been quite astonishing. Kate remembered her suspicions of Jon, her feeling that it was the quiet ones you had to watch. Well, Susan was another quiet one. It was pretty clear that there were plenty of violent feelings boiling away beneath the surface. Had she really tried to cause an accident in the car?

Then there was Jon. He'd been wandering around the darkened square. He could have been the one who attacked Maggie. But why would he do it? He'd had a grudge against Kate because of the fight, but he'd got nothing against Maggie. Except, of course, that she'd left them.

Kate remembered some story about an obsessive teenager in America. He'd kept a grudge book, listing the names of everyone who'd ever upset him. When the book was full he'd started killing them one by one – beginning with those in his immediate family.

By now, Kate realised, she was starting to suspect everyone in the family except little Chrissie.

She tried to get off to sleep, but it didn't work. She found that she was lying half-asleep, half-awake, listening for the sound of soft footsteps approaching her door. Whose footsteps she wasn't quite sure . . .

When she woke up for the third time, heart pounding at some imagined sinister sound, Kate gave up. Not caring if she was being silly or not, she got out of bed, locked her bedroom door and wedged a chair under the handle.

Kate finally managed to drop off to sleep just before dawn. She drifted back to the surface in time to hear Susan coming upstairs with her Sunday morning cup of tea. She had to leap out of bed to move the chair, unlock the door and then leap back into bed to do an artistic waking-up impression as Susan came in.

Susan put the cup of tea on Kate's bedside table. 'Good morning, Kate. Are you awake yet?'

Kate yawned and stretched. 'Just about. I had a pretty disturbed night, couldn't seem to get off for ages.'

Susan perched on the end of the bed. 'I'm not surprised after all that terrible business last night. I just wanted to say how sorry I was.'

Kate took a sip of tea. 'Don't worry. It was just a bit of unreasonable behaviour, way over the top. As Jon said, you're becoming a real Carter at last!'

'I don't know what got into me. I suppose, to be honest, I've always resented Maggie being around so much, and when she accused me like that it all sort of burst out . . .' Susan's voice trailed unhappily away.

She looked so sad that Kate felt really sorry for her.

'Don't worry,' she said consolingly. 'Letting it out probably did you the world of good. In your position, resenting Maggie's a perfectly normal reaction.' Kate hesitated. 'Look, it's not up to me to interfere between you and Dad, but I really don't think you've got anything to worry about. I think you bother Maggie far more than she bothers you.'

Susan looked amazed. 'I do?'

'When she walked out on Dad I think she expected him to come running after her, begging her to come back. Well, he didn't, he found you instead.' Susan looked rather shocked, and Kate went on, 'Don't get me wrong, Maggie's still my mum. I care about her, but I don't have too many illusions about her. Maggie's always felt that she's basically perfect – it's one of her greatest assets. The fact that she could be replaced, and successfully replaced . . . I imagine she finds it pretty hard to take.'

Susan stood up. 'Thanks, Kate, you've made me feel a lot better. I'd better go . . .'

'And I'd better get up,' said Kate.

Susan paused in the doorway. 'As a matter of fact, Maggie called first thing. She's coming round for coffee with Nick, to talk things over.' She made a face. 'Can't say I'm looking forward to it.'

'Don't worry, we'll all stand by you! We Carters stick together.'

Susan smiled and hurried out of the room. Kate reached for her tea and there was a sudden crash. The cup and saucer had fallen from the bedside table. The broken cup lay halfway across the room.

Kate frowned. Maybe she had perched the cup

on the edge of the table without realising and it had tipped off. Maybe she'd knocked the cup off the table without realising it when she reached out for it. Odd that it should have rolled so far from the table though . . .

Frowning, Kate climbed out of bed and looked for something to clean up the mess.

Kate came into the sitting room and found a scene of Sunday morning peace. Her father was sprawled on the sofa with coffee and the Sunday papers. Jon sat in an armchair reading a computer magazine and Chrissie was drawing at a table by the window.

Kate looked round. 'Where's Susan?'

'The sports section didn't come,' said her father. 'She went down to the newsagents to get it for me.'

'Lazy devil,' said Kate.

'I offered,' protested Jack. 'Susan said she felt like a walk.'

Kate looked out of the window. Susan was coming back up the street with a newspaper tucked under her arm. 'Here she is.'

A car turned the curve of the street and sped towards the house.

'Here's Mum and Nick,' said Kate turning away from the window. 'Stand by!'

'No!' screamed Chrissie. 'No!'

Kate swung back towards the window. The car had picked up speed, veered over to the right and was hurtling straight towards the unsuspecting Susan.

EIGHT

There was no time to do anything, no time to shout a warning – scarcely time even to react. They were in the house, the approaching tragedy in the street outside.

Missing Susan by inches, the speeding car mounted the pavement, brushing the edge of Susan's dress, and screeched to a halt, its front wheels inches from the low wall of the front garden.

Jack and Kate were running out of the house by now. As they reached the front steps they saw Maggie jump from the driving seat. She ran up to Susan, who was standing quite still beside the car.

'Susan are you all right? I'm so sorry. The steering must have failed or something.'

Susan stared at her wide-eyed. 'You tried to kill me,' she whispered. 'You deliberately tried to run me down.'

'No, of course not, that's ridiculous,' said Maggie indignantly. 'The car just . . . ran away from me.' She turned to Nick. 'Tell her, Nick.'

Nick gave her a helpless look. 'I dunno, it all happened so fast. You okay, Susan?'

By now Jack was on the scene. He put his arms around Susan who was beginning to shake, and looked angrily at Maggie. 'We know you're the world's worst driver, Maggie, but this is a bit much even for you. You're not safe on the roads.'

'Don't shout at me,' said Maggie.

'Well, how could you do it?' demanded Jack. 'Even you ought to be able to drive up the street and park a car without nearly killing someone!'

'I don't know what happened,' said Maggie hysterically. 'The wheel seemed to twist by itself in my hands; maybe the steering failed. Do you think I tried to run her over on purpose?'

No one answered her.

Kate looked at the car slewed up on the pavement and the distraught group standing beside it. Glancing round she saw that Mrs Pearson was on her front porch and the curtains were twitching along the street.

Kate felt almost hysterical. 'Never a dull moment with the Carters for neighbours,' she said. 'A festival of flying flower pots and crashing cars. Tomorrow, a plague of locusts!'

Jack looked up from comforting Susan. 'It's nothing to make stupid jokes about, Kate. Susan could have been killed.'

'Sorry,' said Kate. 'How about we stop providing the street with free entertainment and go inside? Nick, why don't you park the car? Preferably in the road.'

While Nick reversed the car off the pavement, the rest of them went back to the house. Jon was waiting at the top of the steps.

'Where's Chrissie?' asked Susan.

'Inside, drawing.'

'Was she frightened?'

Jon shrugged. 'Not a bit. She just went on drawing. Maybe she didn't see what was going on.'

'Yes she did,' said Kate. 'She called out.'

Susan ran into the front room. Kate followed and saw that Chrissie was still drawing at the table by the window.

'It's all right, Chrissie,' said Susan. 'Mummy's not hurt.'

Chrissie nodded and went on calmly drawing.

'Why don't you all sit down and get your breath back?' suggested Kate. 'I'll get us all some coffee. Come and give me a hand, will you Nick?'

Nick looked puzzled, but he caught the urgency in her voice and said, 'Yeah, sure . . .'

They went out into the kitchen. Kate put a big tray on the table and said, 'Coffee mugs, milk, sugar, teaspoons, okay? I'll make the coffee.'

Nick groaned. 'Same old bossy boots!'

Feeling that instant coffee didn't quite meet the case, Kate got out the posh French coffee-pot.

She put the kettle on and spooned coffee into the pot. 'Nick, what happened in the car?'

Nick began loading up the tray. 'Search me! We were trundling along in Maggie's usual slap-happy style. One or two near misses on the way, but nothing serious. We came round the curve and saw Susan, and I said, "There's Susan!" or something brilliant like that, and the car sort of – sprang at her.'

Kate gave him a look – it wasn't like Nick to be so fanciful. 'You mean Maggie stepped on the accelerator?'

'I suppose she must have done – but that's honestly not what it felt like. It just sort of – happened. I'll swear Maggie was just as surprised as everyone else.'

'Was there anything wrong with the car when you parked it?'

'Not a thing. I even drove round the block to make sure. The car's fine.'

The electric kettle boiled and clicked off.

Kate poured boiling water onto the coffee. 'I don't think Maggie does care for Susan much. I was telling Susan this morning that she can't bear someone else taking her place – even when it's a place she doesn't want any more. If she was feeling a sort of suppressed rage and it somehow took over . . .'

'Rubbish,' said Nick uneasily. 'I mean we all get murderous impulses from time to time but we don't actually carry them out. Although . . .'

'Although what?'

'You know yesterday evening, when I got nicked?'

'I never did get the full story.'

'Well, I was really – cheesed off, to put it mildly, what with blowing the exams and the row with Dad. Anyway, I went out for a pint.'

'Surprise, surprise!'

'Listen, will you? I had one pint, then I had just enough money for another. The landlord wouldn't serve me, said I was drunk. I felt like smashing him over the head with one of his own bar stools.'

Kate looked at him in alarm. 'But you didn't?'

'Not quite. I went outside and this porky yuppie appeared. Stinking rich, flash car, gorgeous girlfriend. I hated him on sight. He thought I was begging, gave me fifty pence and told me to get a job. That did it!'

'Did what?'

'Next thing I knew I'd grabbed him. I was going to chuck him through the pub window and take his car and his bird. I'd have done it too if those two rozzers hadn't turned up. I might have killed him. And I'll tell you something else. He was a full grown man, and on the heavy side. Kate, I picked him up and waved him like a flag.'

Nick seemed totally baffled by his own actions, and by his sudden surge of strength, thought Kate. As if someone else had been in charge. 'You felt like doing something violent – and suddenly found yourself doing it,' she said slowly. 'Maybe the same thing happened to Maggie.'

Maybe something was taking them all over. Some evil spirit, moving from one mind to another to do its evil work. Kate shivered.

Jon appeared in the doorway, wrenching her back to reality. 'That coffee ready? Conversation's getting a bit sticky in there.'

'I can imagine,' said Kate. She picked up the tray. 'Bring the coffee pot, Nick. Oh and Jon, fetch the biscuit tin will you?'

'Tell you something funny about that incident,' said Jon as he got the biscuits from the cupboard.

Kate paused in the doorway. 'What?'

'Chrissie screamed out "No!" *before* the car speeded up and headed for Susan – as if she knew it was going to happen.'

After everyone had been served with coffee, Jack made a clumsy little speech. 'It's nice to see the family together – both branches, so to speak,' he said awkwardly. 'I mean, we're all civilised people, I hope?

No one disagreed and he ploughed on. 'We all seem to have been having a bad time this weekend, one way and another. Kate and Jon had a dust-up, Kate came off her bike, Nick and I had a row ... I reckon that had a lot to do with Nick's spot of bother afterwards. The row was mostly my fault – sorry Nick!'

It was the first time Jack had ever apologised.

Nick looked embarrassed. 'I'm the one should be sorry. And – thanks for all standing by me. If it wasn't for you lot I'd still be down the nick.' He grinned at Kate. 'Or serving my time on the chain gang!'

'There was that nasty incident in the square,' Jack went on. 'Someone attacking Maggie. Now there's this business this morning, Maggie's car just missing Susan – sheer accident, of course.'

He paused. 'Seems like nothing can go right for this family recently. Like Kate said, "The Curse of the Carters." Anyway, all I want to say is, let's all let bygones be bygones and try to be better friends in the future.'

There was a murmur of agreement, and Jack beamed. Glancing round the room, Kate saw Susan sitting in the corner. Susan wasn't joining in the smiling and murmuring. She looked tired and strained, hair straggling over her face, a smear of grime on her forehead. She was staring fixedly at Maggie.

Maggie sat on the other side of the room, smart and glamorous in a new silk dress, her shining black hair pulled back in a neat pony-tail. The contrast couldn't have been greater. For some reason Kate had a sudden feeling of dread – as if something terrible was about to happen.

The coffee pot exploded.

Maggie, who was nearest to the table it stood on, was showered with hot coffee, coffee-grinds and bits of china. She jumped up with a scream of pain. She was clutching her wrist and blood trickled from a cut above her eye.

There was uproar, with everyone talking at once. Maggie touched her face and saw blood on her fingers. 'I've been cut,' she sobbed. 'I'll be scarred . . .'

Kate's first aid training took over. She jumped up and went over to Maggie, examining the cut. 'It's only a little cut, Mum, we'll soon get it seen to. Is there any more damage?'

'My wrist hurts.'

Kate looked at the wrist which was red and angry-looking. 'Bit of a scald, but it's not too bad.' She raised her voice. 'Anyone else hurt? Any more cuts or scalds?'

Apart from a few coffee splashes everyone else seemed okay.

'Come on, Mum,' said Kate firmly. She took Maggie by the arm and led her upstairs to the bathroom. She cleaned the cut and put a sticking plaster on it. 'That'll heal in a day or so – and there'll be no scar, I promise you.' She ran cold water on the scalded wrist. 'No point in doing anything to that. Let the air get to it and it'll clear up in a couple of days.'

Maggie stared in the mirror, touching the little plaster with her finger. 'I might have been blinded,' she whispered. 'I could have been scarred for life . . .' She began to shiver. 'There's something in this house, Kate. Something evil. I could feel it hating me. It's Susan, I tell you. She was staring at me, just before . . .'

'Don't be so daft,' said Kate. 'Look, there could have been a nasty accident but there wasn't. All you've got is a tiny cut and a minor scald. I'd say you got off pretty lightly. Can't say the same for that dress though.'

The distraction worked. Forgetting her fears and her injuries, Maggie started splashing cold water on the coffee-stained silk.

'I've just bought this dress,' she wailed. 'It's a Balenciaga from the nearly new shop, it cost a fortune. It's ruined!'

Kate perched on the edge of the bath, watching

her. 'Mum, that business with the car – what happened exactly?'

Maggie dabbed at the dress with a sponge. 'I've no idea.' She turned and looked at Kate. 'I was just driving up the street when I saw little Susan trotting along with her newspaper.' Her voice changed, hardened. 'The perfect little housewife – going home to my house and my husband! I suppose I hated her for a moment. Then suddenly the car was on the pavement . . .'

Maggie stood glaring into the mirror, her face distorted with anger. A bottle of Susan's perfume tipped over and rolled from the bathroom shelf into the bath and smashed, filling the room with its light, flowery scent.

For a moment mother and daughter stared at the shattered scent bottle.

'Don't worry, I'll clean it up later,' said Kate. 'I'd better check up on things downstairs. Are you all right?'

Maggie nodded, scrubbing mechanically at the dress.

Kate went back downstairs to the sitting room. Everyone was still talking excitedly about the accident, and gazing at the fragments of the shattered coffee pot. Everyone except Chrissie who was still quietly drawing in the corner. No one, Kate noticed resignedly, was making the slightest effort to clear up the mess.

'How's Mum?' asked Nick.

Her father said, 'Is Maggie all right? Was she hurt?'

'No, she's okay. A small cut and a minor scald.

The main damage was financial. She'll probably sue you.'

'What the hell happened there?' said Jack. 'Did you reheat the coffee-pot in the microwave or something?'

Kate shook her head. 'Just poured in hot water at usual. We've used that pot hundreds of times.'

'Maybe there was some sort of flaw in the pottery,' suggested Susan. 'It suddenly gave way under the heat.'

'Stranger things happen, Dad,' said Jon.

'Like what?'

'Oh, like corn circles and showers of frogs and fish . . .'

His father stared at him. 'Showers of *what*?'

'Unexplained Phenomena,' said Jon solemnly. 'Mysterious events with no natural explanation. You'd be surprised what goes on. I've got this book . . .'

Nick dismissed Jon's ideas with his usual scorn. 'I suppose there are little green men hovering over the house in a UFO? Maybe they powed the coffee-pot with their death-ray!'

Jon's face was white with rage. He'd always hated his big brother's teasing.

'Someone will pow you with a death-ray one of these days Nick,' he said furiously.

Nick laughed. 'Is that a threat, Professor Pie-head? Building one up in your room, are you?'

'Stop it!' shouted Kate. 'Just shut up, both of you!'

Everyone looked at her in surprise.

'You heard what Dad said. We should all try

to be better friends. I shouldn't be surprised if it wasn't all the anger in this family that was causing the trouble.'

'Anger doesn't explode coffee-pots,' objected Nick.

'Don't be too sure,' said Jon quietly. 'You'd be surprised what anger can do. It got you arrested, didn't it?'

Nick looked oddly at him but didn't reply.

Maggie came down from the bathroom. She'd recovered her self-possession, but looked damp and offended. 'I've done all I can but I think I ought to go home and change. Maybe I can find a cleaner who opens on Sundays . . .' She turned to Nick. 'Will you bring me home? I'm feeling a bit shaken by all this.'

'One condition,' said Nick. 'I drive.'

'If you like,' said Maggie loftily. 'Shall we be off then?'

No one argued with her.

'I'm glad you weren't too badly hurt,' said Jack awkwardly. 'You must send me the bill – for having the dress cleaned.'

Nick and Maggie left, and the rest of the Carters waved them goodbye from the doorstep. They went back inside.

'Poor Maggie,' said Jack. 'She's had quite a morning. I don't think we'll be seeing very much of her for a bit.'

Susan said, 'Well, it's an ill wind – ' She broke off, shooting a guilty look at her husband.

Jack gave a roar of laughter. 'I know, love. A little of Maggie goes a very long way – and I've already had more than my share.' He looked round the room. 'Tell you what, we'll go out for a nice drive after lunch, shall we? Somewhere out in the country.'

He looked at Charlie, still placidly drawing and scooped her up, knocking her drawing book to the floor. 'How about it, eh, Chrissie? Fancy a nice drive out to the country to see the sheep and the cows?'

Chrissie's face showed a mixture of panic and delight. She seemed to be fond of her new stepfather, but found his size, and his noisiness, a bit overpowering.

Jack passed Chrissie over to Susan and said, 'What about you two?'

'Well, actually – ' Kate and Jon both spoke together, then stopped, looking at each other wryly. If there was one thing they both hated, it was a nice Sunday-afternoon drive in the country with the family.

'Look,' said Kate, 'Jon and I have both got things to do. You and Susan and Chrissie go, get away from it all. I'll get supper.'

After a lot more discussion – for some reason there *always* had to be a lot more discussion with family plans – Kate's suggestion was agreed. Jack, Susan and Chrissie set off in the family car straight after lunch. Jon and Kate volunteered to do the washing-up so they could get away earlier.

Jon and Kate got on with the washing-up. They worked in silence for a while, until Jon said, 'You know when you told Dad we both had things to do?'

Kate shrugged. 'Just the usual vague excuse. Why, you didn't want to go did you?'

Jon shook his head. 'The thing is, Kate, it wasn't just an excuse. We have got something to do, something vitally important. We've got to find out what's attacking this family – and stop it before it's too late.'

NINE

'Attacking?' said Kate. 'Come off it, that's ridiculous.'

But she knew it wasn't.

Jon said, 'Something weird's happening. You know it as well as I do.' He sploshed a plate into the washing up bowl.

They finished the washing up, made themselves instant coffee and took it into the sitting room.

'All right,' said Kate. 'You start.'

Jon stared at her for a moment, eyes gleaming behind his glasses. 'You still don't trust me, do you? Do you really think I'm causing all this trouble?'

'I don't know,' said Kate wearily. 'I did at first. About my bike accident I mean. But so much else has happened since . . . I don't see how you could be doing it all.'

Jon leaned forward. 'Kate, I give you my word I'm not. And I told you the absolute truth about that bike business. I gave you a couple of flat tyres and that's it. I didn't touch your brakes – I'll swear it on anything you like.'

Kate drew a deep breath. 'Okay, I'll believe you – if you'll believe I didn't trash your room.'

'I know. Did I tell you nothing was stolen after all? When I got things sorted out everything was there.'

'So much for Dad's teenage burglar,' said Kate. 'So if there wasn't a burglar and I didn't do it – and I didn't – who did?'

For a moment Jon didn't answer. Then he said, 'When I tidied up, I noticed the mess was laid out in a kind of circular pattern – as if there'd been a tornado inside the room.'

Kate suddenly felt cold. There it was again – the feeling of something unnatural, inexplicable. The fear of the unknown.

'How do you explain that then?' she asked uneasily.

'All I've got is a theory. Before I can explain it, you're going to have to believe two things – or at least go along with them, for the time being.'

'What's impossible thing number one?'

'That things happen in the world which just can't be explained – at least, not in the everyday scientific way.'

'Such as?'

Jon fished a paperback from the back pocket of his jeans. 'Such as the sort of stuff in here. It's that book I was talking about.'

'What's it about?'

'Ghosts, UFOs, telepathy, ESP, poltergeists, corn circles, Uri Geller, warning dreams, witchcraft, everything from the Abominable Snowman to the Loch Ness Monster.'

'Quite a list. What about evidence?'

'There are documented reports on all of them, evidence, eyewitnesses, the lot. Even photographs.'

'Faked photographs – and stories by a lot of loonies.'

Jon gritted his teeth in exasperation. 'All right, some of these things could be delusions or frauds, I expect some of them are – but *all* of them? Every single one – out of hundreds of cases?'

'What's the second thing I need to believe?'

'Someone's using some kind of unknown force against this family. Someone who hates the family and wants to destroy it.'

'Got it!' said Kate. 'Mrs P next door is head of the local witchcraft circle and she's trying to scare us into moving away.'

Jon didn't laugh. 'You're doing it again.'

'Am I? Doing what?'

'Trying to deny what's happening, trying to – to joke it out of existence.' He pointed to the still-damp remains of the coffee stains on the wall and on the rug. 'Kate, you and I *saw* something impossible happen, right here in this room just a few hours ago. We all did. Nothing normal or natural or reasonable made that coffee pot explode. Yet we fudge up some explanation about microwaves or pottery fatigue – when we've just *seen* something that breaks every natural law. Seen it and ignored it – because our minds just can't take it in!'

Kate didn't answer. There didn't seem anything to say. She had a terrible feeling that Jon was right. If he was, the implications were terrifying. How did you fight the supernatural?

'Just before that,' Jon went on, 'we saw our own mother apparently trying to murder Susan, and we hardly even *mention* that – far too embarrassing! I know Mum always goes way over the top, but I don't see her as a cold-blooded killer, do you?'

'No, of course not.'

Jon leaned forward. 'But it *happened*, didn't it? Susan could easily have been killed. Like you, when your brakes failed, or Nick, when that flower pot just missed him. Unless we get this sorted out, the next accident might be a fatal one. One of us could die.' He drew a deep breath, sat back and looked challengingly at her. 'No jokes, Kate?'

'No jokes,' said Kate. She made a determined attempt to control her fears. 'You said you had a theory?'

Jon waved the book at her. 'A common thread runs thought a lot of stuff in this book. Things being made to happen by mental energy – psychic energy if you like. Poltergeists chuck things about, Uri Geller bends spoons, witches clobber their enemies. All done with the power of the mind. Scientists reckon the rituals, all the chanting and dancing and sacrifices and all that don't actually do anything at all. It's just a way to hype up the psychic energy-levels. With me so far?'

'Just about.'

'So look at the amount of mental energy flying

about in this family. Dad's got a hell of a temper, Nick's just the same, Maggie's incredibly strong-willed – and you're pretty quick to fly off the handle yourself.'

'What about you?'

'I'm the worst kind,' said Jon calmly. 'Nothing on the surface and everything bubbling away inside. It's people like me who get a rifle, climb the nearest water-tower and start picking off passers-by at random.'

'You're not as bad as all that,' said Kate. 'You're quite loveable sometimes.' All the same, she realised guiltily, Jon was simply echoing her own thoughts about him.

'Susan's like me,' said Jon. 'Lots of fierce feelings, all bottled up. She hates Maggie and she's hell-bent on hanging on to Dad.'

'Okay,' said Kate. 'You've made your point – there's plenty of strong emotion flying around in the Carter family circle. *But there always has been*. Why's it suddenly producing all these weird goings-on?'

'Exactly,' said Jon. 'When all it ought to produce is the sort of thing we're all used to – lots of rows and fights, a few thrown dinner plates and a divorce.'

'Just normal family life in other words. What's changed?'

'Something's taking all this mental energy and turning it against us.'

'That's a bit much, Jon, surely?'

'Is it? Let's go right back to the beginning. You borrowed my sweater, right? All right, all

94

right, I know you didn't trash my room. *But I bet you thought about doing it?*'

'No, of course not,' said Kate indignantly. 'I wouldn't – ' She broke off as something tugged at her memory.

'Yes I did,' she whispered. 'I couldn't find my own sweater because my own room was such a mess. I thought about your room all neat and tidy and I had a sudden impulse to trash it, to make it no better than mine. But I didn't *do* it . . .'

'Something did. Something that took the thought and the evil energy from your mind and made it happen.'

Kate sat back, her mind filled with horror. If every bad thought, every evil impulse was to become real . . .

'Don't you see,' said Jon, '*It was the same with me*! When I went down to the bike shed, I actually *thought* about sabotaging your brakes so you'd have a real accident. But I didn't *do* it. I just gave you the punctures. Something took that impulse from my mind – '

'And used it to snap both my brake cables when I was shooting down the hill? Come on, Jon!'

'It happened, though, didn't it?' said Jon. 'It affects the way we behave as well. When I saw my room wrecked I wanted to hit you – and suddenly I did. When you gave me that nosebleed I felt like throttling you – and found myself doing it.'

'Like the way that row between Dad and Nick

turned really nasty,' said Kate. 'Dad felt like chucking that pot at Nick – and somehow it happened!'

Jon nodded. 'Later on Nick was so angry he felt like murdering someone – and he nearly did!'

'What about Maggie being attacked in the square?'

'I've got a theory about that, too. I reckon Susan was steamed up about Dad running off whenever Maggie snapped her fingers. As she walked through that dark square she thought about Maggie being mugged – and it happened!'

'So who attacked her?'

'I don't know,' said Jon irritably. 'Some kind of astral projection maybe . . .'

'Susan was so furious with Dad that she felt like wrecking the car on the way home,' said Kate. 'That nearly happened too.'

'Same thing happened today,' said Jon. 'Maggie's driving along, sees Susan, has an evil impulse – and all of a sudden the car's halfway up the pavement.'

'And the coffee pot?'

Jon shrugged. 'Susan annoyed about nearly getting run over, resenting how smart Maggie always looks, wanting something had to happen to her – and pow! Don't you see Kate, it all hangs together.'

In a way it did, thought Kate. But by the standards of every day life it was total lunacy. Only – what was the alternative?

'So, who's doing all this? Some enemy we don't know about? Someone Dad's upset?'

Jon shook his head. 'The whole thing's too personal. I think it's someone in the family. I think it's one of us.'

'So it could be me – or you?'

'That's right.'

It was a shocking idea. But somehow Kate couldn't help feeling that Jon was right.

'Supposing this is all true – how do we find which one of us is doing all this and make them stop?'

Jon stood up. 'I haven't got that far yet. I've just provided the question. I hoped you'd come up with the answer!'

'Thanks a lot!' Kate stood up as well. 'Let's have a look at that book of yours, maybe it'll give me some ideas.'

Jon passed over the paperback. 'I'll go through some of my other books, I might find something useful.'

Kate put her hands on his bony shoulders. 'I'll tell you something this evil force of yours doesn't realise. We Carters may hate each other some-times, but we love each other too. That's how we'll beat this thing.' She gave him a quick hug and kissed him on the cheek.

Jon's ears turned bright pink and he fled from the room.

Kate sat down again, the book in her hands, thinking over their strange conversation. Already it was beginning to seem unreal. But Jon was right. Was it any more unreal than the way they'd all ignored what was happening under their noses?

She began leafing through the book. It was full of strange things and inexplicable events. Disappearing planes, ships found deserted, their crews vanished. Showers of frogs and fishes in the desert. People who just burst into flames – spontaneous combustion that was called. Invisible stone throwers smashing every window in a house. People who were kidnapped by flying saucers, who dreamed of forthcoming disasters or got phone calls from dead relatives. Some of it was scary, some of it just plain silly, but it was all undeniably weird.

The nearest thing to their own experiences was the many stories concerning poltergeists. The word apparently means 'noisy ghosts' and these spirits certainly lived up to their name. They slammed doors, smashed windows, threw stones, food, furniture and crockery through the air. Like incredibly bad children they smashed things, made noises and made a mess.

The trashing of Jon's room looked a bit like poltergeist activity. So did some of the minor breakages and disturbances. But the things she was really worried about, the dangerous 'accidents' all seemed too personal and planned, too clearly directed against someone in the family. Poltergeists seemed to go in for random mischief, not aimed at anyone in particular. Maybe they'd got a super poltergeist, one that thought and planned. Would they have to move? If they did, would it follow them?

Apparently poltergeists were associated with disturbed adolescent girls. 'I suppose that makes me the prime suspect,' thought Kate.

She felt a tide of fear welling up inside her, a mad impulse to run screaming out of the house. 'And a lot of good that would do,' she told herself angrily. 'Get a grip on yourself, Kate!' She stood up and paced about the room, trying to control her fears and form some kind of plan.

Glancing out of the window, she saw a man wandering up the street, looking at each house in turn. His hair was wild and straggly, he needed a shave and his sports jacket and flannels were shabby and threadbare. She wondered if he was a beggar or a burglar but decided he was neither, though his thin face with its big, dark eyes had something strange about it, something furtive and shifty. The funny thing was, he looked familiar . . .

The man stopped outside the house, and saw Kate watching him through the window. He looked back at her with an intent, penetrating stare. Then he climbed the front steps and rang the doorbell.

'Now what?' thought Kate. 'Sinister strangers on top of everything else? He can just clear off.'

The doorbell rang again.

Reluctantly Kate went to the front door. She put on the door-chain and opened the door just a crack. 'Yes?'

The stranger stood on the doorstep, peering through the gap. 'I was looking for Susan – Susan

Carter it would be now. Do I have the right address?'

'Yes, you do, but I'm afraid she's out for a drive with my father. I'm Kate Carter.'

'I'm Kevin Lovelle, Susan's ex-husband. Chrissie's father.'

TEN

The man gave her an ingratiating smile. 'You probably don't remember, but we met briefly. You and Susan were shopping in the high street.'

That was where she'd seen the man before! He'd come up to them, and Susan had introduced him. She'd seemed a bit embarrassed but maybe that was only natural. Then she'd just sent Kate on into the greengrocers to buy fruit. By the time Kate had come out the man was gone.

'Will Susan be long?' asked Kevin Lovelle politely. 'I do need to see her rather urgently.'

Kate knew all about not letting strange men in the house. And there was something odd about this stranger, for all his polite manners. Something that made her flesh creep. All the same, you couldn't leave your stepmother's ex-husband standing on the doorstep, could you? It wasn't as if she was alone in the house, Jon was up in his room.

Kate decided she'd have to risk it. 'They should be back any minute now. Would you like to come in and wait?'

'If you're sure it's no trouble.'

'Not at all. You don't mind sitting in the kitchen?'

'My favourite room!' There was something overdone about the man's manner. He was flogging the charm a bit too much. And he was staring fixedly at her in a way she didn't like. It occurred to Kate that she didn't know why Susan had divorced him, only that the separation had been painful and unpleasant. For all she knew the man was a dangerous psychopath. Still, it was too late now. She took him into the kitchen and sat him down at the table.

'Would you like a cup of coffee? Only instant, I'm afraid, our pot got smashed this morning.'

Kate saw the man's eyes open wide. 'Instant will be fine. What happened to your coffee pot? Somebody drop it?'

'No, it just exploded.'

'How very alarming!'

There was something off-key about the man's reaction – not so much surprised as secretly pleased. Kate had a sudden, terrifying thought. If the unknown enemy was an outsider with a reason to hate the Carter family, Kevin Lovelle was the perfect candidate. As far as he was concerned, her father must seem like the man who had stolen his wife and child. Kevin Lovelle had every reason to hate the Carters – and to want revenge.

So what was he doing here now?

Perhaps he was checking up on the effects of his evil spell, or curse or tame poltergeist or whatever it was. Or maybe he'd come to make another attack, finish someone off.

Kate made him a cup of instant coffee and

handed it over. His hand trembled as he took the cup.

Kate suddenly noticed the long gleaming knife on the draining board. She thought about snatching it up, then told herself she was being paranoid. She filled a bowl with water and began washing lettuce for the salad.

'You don't mind if I get on with this, do you Mr Lovelle?'

'Not at all, my dear. And please, call me Kevin. If I may, I'll call you Kate. Always first names in the profession, you know.'

'The profession – oh, I see you're an *actor*!' She did her best to sound impressed. Better keep him in in a good humour. 'That must be fascinating work.'

'When there is any work, Kate. Ninety per cent unemployment in the good times – and these are the bad times. Only the odd voiceover keeps body and soul together. Dog food and dandruff shampoo commercials mostly!' He took a sip of coffee. 'Have there been any more of these strange events – like your explosive coffee pot, I mean?' He tried to sound casual but there was eager interest in his voice.

'Quite a few actually,' said Kate. 'Why, are you interested in that sort of thing?'

'I've studied the field a little, just as a hobby you understand.'

'Maybe you can give us some good advice. We've had rooms wrecked, heavy stone flowerpots flying through the air, bikes and cars going out of control, all sorts of things.'

'And how long has all this been going on?'

'Just this weekend.'

'How terrible for you! There was something false, almost gloating about his concern. 'Susan and Chrissie must be very upset.'

'Susan seems to be coping pretty well. And it's hard to tell what Chrissie thinks about things,'

He nodded sympathetically. 'Still not talking?'

'No.'

Kevin sat sipping his coffee. Kate couldn't help feeling he was somehow pleased at what she'd been telling him. Maybe her theory was right after all. Maybe he was behind their troubles. If he was, how could she catch him out?

Kate watched him as she put lettuce into a salad bowl. She got out the remains of the beef and picked up the big carving knife. The man's eyes seemed to follow the long gleaming blade . . .

To Kate's huge relief, there came the sound of a car drawing up and a door slamming. 'That sounds like Dad and Susan.'

The front door opened and closed and a moment later Susan appeared, a sleeping Chrissie in her arms. 'We've had a lovely time, Chrissie's quite worn out. Your father's just gone for petrol – ' She broke off at the sight of the figure at the table.

Kevin Lovelle stood up. 'Susan, my dear! And little Chrissie! I hope this isn't too much of a shock?'

It was quite obvious from Susan's manner that it was a shock – and a very unpleasant one too.

'Hello, Kevin,' she said quietly. 'Kate, would

you take Chrissie and put her on her bed. Just lay her down as she is, I'll get her ready for bed later.'

Putting down the knife, Kate took the sleeping child, carried her upstairs, and laid her gently on her bed. Chrissie stirred but didn't wake.

As she came back downstairs she heard Kevin saying, 'A touch of the old trouble then? Sorry to hear that.'

'Don't upset me, Kevin,' said Susan in a cold, hard voice. 'Not if you know what's good for you. Or have you forgotten?'

Kate went into the kitchen. 'She's still fast –'

'Kate, will you excuse us for a moment?' said Susan.

It was a tone Kate had never heard her use before and her face was hard and set. Kate looked at Kevin Lovelle and abandoned any thought of him as a black magic mastermind. His face was white and he was trembling. It was quite clear that he was terrified – and that it was Susan he was afraid of.

'Susan?' thought Kate, as she went into the front room. 'Not Susan, surely . . .'

As she stood looking out of the window Kate could hear low, angry voices from the kitchen.

Kevin was saying '. . . wouldn't bother you unless it was urgent.'

She heard Susan say something about, 'Urgent for the feathers.'

Kate frowned. Feathers? Were they discussing some sinister black magic ritual? Ridiculous, she told herself, but still . . .

The car drew up outside and her father jumped out. Kate went to the door to warn him, but he gave her a quick kiss and rushed straight past her.

'Dad, wait!' she called.

Jack didn't stop. He went straight to the kitchen with Kate trailing behind. They both arrived in time to see Susan give Kevin a little bundle of notes from her purse.

'Well, well, well,' said Jack Carter. 'Introduce me, Susan.'

Susan looked upset, but she spoke in a quiet firm voice.

'This is Kevin Lovelle, my ex-husband. Kevin, this is Jack Carter.'

'Delighted to meet you,' said Kevin, hurriedly tucking the money out of sight. 'Sorry I have to rush.'

Jack stood blocking the doorway. 'You mustn't think of leaving yet. I've been hoping to meet you for ages.'

Kevin gave him a quick look. 'You surprise me.'

'Oh yes,' said Jack. 'I was particularly keen to have a word with you when Susan first came to work for me, before we were married. Some difficulty about your maintenance payments for Susan and Chrissie. There weren't any – and you were nowhere to be found.'

'There were a few problems,' said Kevin airily. 'I was working abroad. All sorted out now. Well, I must be off . . .'

Jack spoke with a sinister jollity. 'You know, I

don't think you've quite got the idea yet. You're supposed to give Susan money, not the other way round. So we'll have that cash she just gave you back, shall we?'

'Jack, leave it,' said Susan wearily. 'Let him go!'

Kate could see that her father's formidable temper was rising. She could sense Kevin Lovelle's fear and anger too – and his fierce determination not to give up the money.

A plate suddenly flew out of the kitchen cupboard and smashed against the opposite wall. Kate jumped and Susan gave a little gasp. Locked in concentration on each other the two men didn't even notice.

All at once Kate realised Jon was right. *Something* was taking the anger in the room and magnifying it to the point of madness.

'It's happening again,' thought Kate. 'Only worse!'

Jack advanced on Kevin Lovelle who backed away. He edged sideways towards the table as if to dodge around his bigger opponent. Jack moved too, blocking his escape.

Cupboard doors banged open and cups and plates flew across the room. Nobody took any notice.

Kate put her hand on her father's shoulder. 'Dad, please . . .'

The muscles in his back were bunched rock-hard, and he was vibrating with tension. He shook off her hand and stepped forward. 'Give me that money you little rat!'

Kevin snatched up the carving-knife from beside the joint of cold beef. The long blade gleamed in the afternoon sunlight.

'Keep back!'

Kate gasped. Jack took great pride in that carving-knife, sharpening it before every meal. The blade was razor-sharp.

'Dad, be careful!' she screamed.

Ignoring her, Jack leaped forward, grappling with Kevin. The blade flashed and there was a spattering of blood. Suddenly Jack's white sports-shirt had a spreading scarlet stain across the chest. The two men were fighting for possession of the knife, locked together like statues. Blood was pouring from a gash in Jack's ear.

Ignoring the wound, Jack tightened his grip on the smaller man's wrist. He turned the blade of the knife away from his face until it was pointing downwards towards Kevin's own throat. He began forcing the knife blade lower, until it was inches from Kevin's neck.

Kate could see the artery in Kevin's neck pulsing with effort. If the edge of the blade touched the swelling artery a fountain of blood would spring out. For one fierce moment Kate actually seemed to see the knife slice home, and the spurting blood. She had to stop them or Kevin would be dead in a matter of minutes, and her father would be a murderer.

Susan screamed and hurled herself at the two men but she was too small to make any impact. She simply bounced off them and fell back sobbing.

Kate looked round for something, anything that might help. She saw the bowl of cold water on the draining board, the one she'd been using to wash the lettuce. Wriggling past the two struggling men she grabbed the bowl and hurled the cold water over them both.

Jack gave a bellow of rage and loosened his grip on the other man's arm from sheer shock. Kevin dropped the knife and darted out of the door. His feet pounded down the hall and the front door slammed behind him.

A wailing cry came from upstairs. Not surprisingly, Chrissie had been woken up by all the noise.

'Go and see to her,' said Kate. 'I'll look after Dad.'

Susan disappeared and Kate turned to her father.

He was an extraordinary sight. Soaked in blood and water, and decorated with the odd lettuce leaf he stood swaying in the middle of the kitchen.

Kate put a kitchen chair behind him and shoved him down on it. He was still bleeding freely from the cut in his ear. She got a clean drying-up cloth from the linen drawer, folded it into a pad and gave it to him.

'Here, hold this to your ear. Press hard.'

He looked at her with the dazed expression of a man coming out of a trance. 'Damn it, Kate, why did you chuck water over me?'

'Well it works on dog-fights,' said Kate shakily.

He looked round the kitchen. 'But he got away . . .'

Kate picked up the bloodstained carving knife from the floor.

'Dad, you were fighting over this – and you had it right at his throat. You nearly killed him.'

Kate saw the shock spread over her father's face as he realised what might so easily have happened.

'I wanted to kill him,' he said. 'I wanted to slit his throat. I've – never felt like that before.'

He sat down at the kitchen table looking stunned. Kate got the big first-aid box from the kitchen cupboard, washed the cut in mild disinfectant, and sprinkled on disinfectant powder. Then she fixed a wad of lint on his ear with big strips of sticking plaster.

'There you go, that should hold it for a while. Maybe you ought to go down to Casualty.'

'On a Sunday night? You could sit there with your head in your lap and still have to wait for hours. I'll get it fixed properly in the morning. Thanks, Kate, you're a treasure.'

She gave him a towel and he started drying his water-soaked hair. As she finished packing away the first-aid kit, Jon came into the kitchen. 'What's been going on? More trouble?' He looked at his bloodstained father. 'What happened to you?'

'Cut myself shaving.'

Jon gave Kate a worried look. 'Is he all right?'

'I think he's still in shock!' said Kate. She started picking up the smashed cups and plates and putting them in the bin. 'So what *happened*?'

'Susan's ex-husband called and things turned nasty,' said Kate. 'Tell you all about it later.'

Jon wasn't satisfied. 'Nasty? Nasty how?'

Suddenly Kate snapped. 'There was a fight over a knife and Dad nearly killed him if you must know. We're lucky we haven't got a dead body on the floor and a father under arrest . . .'

She broke off, fighting back tears.

Her father got up and put an arm round her shoulders. 'All right, Kate, all right. Look, we've all had a bit of a shock. Strong sweet tea, that's what we need. I'll make it . . .'

'I'll do it,' said Kate, sniffing hard. 'You sit down before you fall down.'

Jon put the kettle on, they finished clearing up and Kate made tea. Susan came running down as she was pouring it out.

'Sorry, took me ages to settle Chrissie. Are you all right Jack, is the cut bad? Should we get a doctor?'

'It's only a scratch. Kate's fixed me up fine.'

'I'm sorry about what happened. Kevin's not usually violent.'

Kate pointed accusingly at her father. 'No, but he is!'

Susan looked shocked, as she always did when Kate spoke up to her father, but Jack nodded. 'Kate's right, it was all my fault. If I'd let him go he'd have scuttled off with no trouble. As it was . . .' He shuddered. 'Like Kate said, it's lucky I'm not down the nick on a manslaughter charge.'

Kate poured Susan a cup of tea, and she sat down to join them. 'It's like some old British war movie,' thought Kate. 'Stiff upper lip all round and a nice cuppa solves every problem.'

Susan suddenly became aware of her husband's gory state. 'Look at you Jack! That shirt's covered with blood. You'd better get those clothes off and have a shower. I'll find you a clean shirt.'

Leaving Susan fussing over her father, Kate caught Jon's eye and they went into the sitting room. She told him all about Kevin's visit, and about the fight.

'Fits the pattern, doesn't it?' said Jon, 'All that flying crockery . . . It's definitely a poltergeist.'

'I'm not sure,' said Kate. 'There was something odd going on earlier between Kevin and Susan. The funny thing is, he was terrified of her. He was taunting her, but he was still dead scared.'

'Scared of *Susan*?'

Kate nodded. 'I think Susan's the key to all this. Nothing like this ever happened before she came – and Jack and Maggie had enough rows . . .' She paced up and down for a moment, thinking about what she'd overheard. That stuff about feathers . . .

Suddenly she had a thought. 'Listen Jon, I may have to slip out for a while. I want you to keep an eye on Susan. Hang around and be helpful – and be nice!'

'Why?'

'Because it might not be safe to upset her.'

'All right,' said Jon. As he turned to go his foot kicked something on the floor. It was Chrissie's drawing pad. He picked it up and handed it

Kate. 'Better look after it, she'll want it when she wakes up.'

Jon went out of the room, and Kate stood holding the drawing book, idly leafing through it, glancing at the drawings.

Suddenly she gasped and her heart began to pound. The kaleidoscope in her mind twisted violently and the final pattern formed.

She knew the answer at last.

ELEVEN

Kate stood quite still for a moment. 'Well, most of the answer,' she thought. She needed more information, and there was only one place to get it. She went to the phone and dialled Nick's number. After several rings a sleepy voice answered, 'Yeah?'

'Nick, it's Kate. I need your help. Does "The Feathers" mean anything to you?'

'What feathers?'

'*The* Feathers, you twit. As in pub.'

There was a moment's silence. Then Nick said, 'Yeah, I know it. Ratty little wine bar place down by the station, corner of Coley Street. Sells rotten wine and rotgut spirits, but it's all dead cheap. Real boozer's paradise.'

'Thanks Nick, I knew I could rely on your expert knowledge.'

'Hang on, you're not thinking of going there are you? That place is dangerous, most of the customers are permanently out of their skulls.'

'Me, go to a place like that? Wouldn't think of it!'

Slamming the phone down on Nick's protests, Kate headed for the front door. She slipped into her raincoat and reached for the front door handle. A thought struck her and she turned and went quietly up stairs to her bedroom.

Rummaging in the top shelf of her wardrobe she unearthed the old tin box containing her holiday fund and counted out the little pile of crumpled notes. Thirty-five quid. It would have to do. Stuffing the notes into the back pocket of her jeans she went quietly downstairs and crept out of the house.

The sun was going down leaving a sultry oppressive twilight with a rumble of thunder in the air. Kate hurried down the shadowy street towards the brightly-lit high street, and caught a bus to the station.

'The Feathers' lived up to Nick's description. It was a long thin place shaped very much like a railway carriage with wooden booths down each side and a bar at the far end.

Kate hovered uncertainly outside. She'd hoped for a busy pub where she could slip in unnoticed, but the gloomy, cavernous bar was still half-empty. As soon as she stepped through the door she would face the scrutiny of the occupants of the booths and a tough-looking brute of a barman.

A big hand gripped her arm, she swung round – and saw Nick, just as she'd done outside the police station.

'Stop doing that to me,' she said irritably. 'What are you doing here anyway, this place looks a bit low even for you!'

'Looking for you. I knew you were coming here, I always know when you're lying.'

'I'm glad you're here.'

'Well, what are you up to now?'

'I'm looking for someone. It's a bit of a long shot, but there's a possibility he'll be here.'

'Who?'

'No time to explain. Let's go in and look. If we find him, just take your cue from me. Look thuggish and menacing, that shouldn't be too hard.'

'Right. Hang on, I'm skint.'

Kate sighed, fished in her back pocket and gave him a fiver.

They went inside the wine lodge, their feet echoing on the bare wooden floor. Well, almost bare. Kate had heard her father refer to particularly scruffy pubs as 'spit and sawdust joints.' Now she understood why.

Kate and Nick made their way to the bar and waited while the barman served a wizened old lady with a 'double double champagne'. This turned out to be a pint glass nearly filled with a greenish-yellow fluid that looked like battery acid. Kate was almost sure she saw smoke coming off the top.

'Speciality of the House,' muttered Nick. 'Draft champagne. Don't touch it on any account.' He ordered a bottle of lager and a coke for Kate.

'She of age?' growled the barman.

Nick tossed Kate's fiver on the bar. 'What do you care?'

The barman served them and Nick scooped up the change.

116

They stood at the bar for a moment looking around.

'Is he here?' whispered Nick.

Kate glanced round and felt she'd never seen a more sinister place in her life. None of the traditional pub jollity here, no laughter and chat. Just gloom and semi-darkness and shapeless figures huddled over their glasses. 'The Feathers' was the end of the line.

'Don't think so, maybe it's too early. Yes! There he is!' Kevin Lovelle sat huddled in one of the booths.

'Perfect,' said Kate. 'You sit next to him so he can't get out, I'll sit opposite.'

They strolled up to the booth and pounced, Nick wedging onto the bench beside Kevin and Kate slipping into the seat opposite.

Kevin was staring into the depths of a large whisky. It took him a moment or two to register that they were there.

'Hello, Kevin,' said Kate sternly. She'd read somewhere that the police always used first names to establish dominance. 'You remember, me, Kate Carter? We met this afternoon.'

Kevin looked up. 'I remember you, and I remember your father,' he said in faintly slurred tones. 'Though not with any great pleasure. What do you want?'

'Information,' said Kate. 'About this.' She took the little drawing book from under her coat.

'No,' said Kevin hoarsely. He tried to get up but Nick put a big hand on his shoulder and shoved him down.

'I won't say anything about her,' whispered Kevin. 'It's too dangerous. Several times she nearly killed me, do you know that?'

'She nearly killed us all,' said Kate. 'It's got to stop. That's why you've got to talk.'

Kevin just shook his head. He was clearly terrified.

Kate knew her only chance was to make sure that he was even more frightened of her. She twisted her face into a threatening scowl. 'You've got two choices. This is my brother, Nick. As you can see, he's even bigger and more bad-tempered than my father.'

She kicked her brother under the table and he glared menacingly at Kevin. 'That's right,' he snarled.

'Now then,' Kate went on. 'Either Nick takes you home for another little session with Dad – who still owes you for that slice on the ear, by the way . . .' Kate took the little wad of notes from her back pocket. 'Or you tell me all you can, take this twenty-five quid and disappear.'

Kevin stared eagerly at the money – converting it into large whiskies no doubt, thought Kate. Then he shook his head. 'Not enough, I want fifty . . .'

'This is all there is, so make your mind up. It's an easy twenty-five quid or a social evening with the Carter family. Talk and you can just clear off afterwards. You'll be safe as long as you stay away from us.'

Kevin didn't reply. Kate nodded to Nick who

grabbed Kevin's arm and started heaving him up. No one took any notice.

'All right,' said Kevin, wriggling free. 'But I'll only tell you. Not him.'

'Wait by the door, Nick, will you?' said Kate. 'There's only one way out, isn't there?' Just to be sure she slipped into the place next to Kevin as soon as Nick moved. 'All right,' she said. 'Start talking.'

Kate was silent and thoughtful when she rejoined Nick outside the wine bar. They started walking towards her bus stop. The sky was dark and heavy drops of rain were starting to fall.

'Are you going to tell me what this is all about?' asked Nick.

'Yes, but not now, later tonight. Nick, you've got to fetch Maggie round to our place – this evening, after supper.'

'I'll try, but I doubt if she'll come.'

'Tell her there's going to be a big revelation – about Susan. Hint that it's something really shocking. That'll fetch her if anything will!'

'I'll do my best.'

Kate took his arm. 'You've got to be there, Nick, both of you. I think I can see a way to put a stop to all this trouble we've been having. But it's going to take the whole family . . .'

Everything was peaceful for once when Kate got back home.

The others had had their supper but they'd left her some cold meat and salad, which she ate in the kitchen.

When she'd finished she joined her father, Susan and Jon in the sitting room where they were all watching television. Her father had showered and changed. Apart from the slightly comic patched-up ear he looked absolutely normal.

'Where did you disappear to?' he asked.

'I felt like some fresh air, so I popped round to see Nick.'

Which was true, as far as it went.

She sat for a while, watching television with the others, not really taking anything in. The threatened storm had arrived and wind howled around the house, whipping the heavy rain against the window panes. Kate struggled with a rising sense of dread, worrying about what she was about to do. It could be very dangerous for all of them – but there was no other way.

Just as the news was finishing the doorbell rang.

Jack frowned. 'Who the hell comes visiting on a night like this?'

'I'll go,' said Kate.

She got up and ran to the front door, returning a few seconds later with Nick and Maggie.

Susan jumped up. 'What a nice surprise!'

Jon looked thoughtfully at the new arrivals but didn't speak.

Jack just scowled at them.

There was something formal about the visitors. Nick was wearing clean jeans and a clean T-shirt, which was about as neat as he ever got, and Maggie was looking glamorous in a smart suit.

'What's the matter with your ear, Jack?' said Maggie.

'He cut himself shaving,' said Jon. 'In the kitchen with a carving knife.'

Maggie looked blankly at him.

'Would anyone like a cup of tea?' said Susan. 'Coffee?'

Maggie shook her head. 'Nothing, thank you. Could we just get on with it, please?'

'Get on with what?' asked Jack irritably. 'What's this all about?'

'You tell me,' said Maggie. 'When Nick dragged me round here – very much against my will, I had other plans – he gave me to understand that I was to hear some important piece of family news. Something concerning Susan, he said. Not bad news I hope?'

Jack Carter glared at his son. 'Well, Nick?'

Nick shrugged helplessly and looked appealingly at Kate.

Kate drew a deep breath and stood up. 'Actually, *I* asked Nick to bring Maggie round here. And there is some important news. About what's been happening to us all recently.'

'Do we have to rake all that up again, Kate?' asked her father angrily. 'Can't we have a bit of peace for once?'

'If we keep pretending nothing's happening, the trouble will go on,' said Kate firmly.

'We may have had a few family upsets recently – '

Kate lost patience. 'Upsets! You nearly killed a man a few hours ago. Only yesterday you nearly

121

smashed Nick's head in. Jon and I nearly slaughter each other. Nick attacks a perfect stranger, something weird attacks Maggie, Maggie tries to mow down Susan, the coffee-pot blows up – and you talk about upsets! What does it take to wake you up?'

Her father just stared, astonished at her outburst. Suddenly Kate felt the tension in the room building up, as if her outburst had triggered something off.

Jack jumped to his feet, his face red with anger. 'All right, some weird things have been going on, I admit it. But what's the point of upsetting everyone by raking over it all again?'

A china vase jumped from the mantelpiece and smashed in the fireplace.

'It's starting,' thought Kate.

'Kate, what is all this about?' demanded Maggie. 'Have you got something to tell us or not?'

Kate raised her voice. 'This afternoon, Susan's ex-husband came round. He got some money from Susan, even though he was frightened of her. Then Dad came home, there was a fight and Kevin ran off. This evening Nick and I went to see him, in a pub called "The Feathers".'

'You went to "The Feathers"?' roared Jack. 'Nick, what the hell are you thinking of, taking her there?'

Nick shrugged. 'She took me.'

Ignoring them, Kate continued. 'Kevin was still scared, but he needed money. I bribed him and he told me certain things – about his marriage to Susan.'

Susan jumped up. 'Kate, please no . . .'

'What the hell do you think you're doing, Kate?' demanded her father. 'You've got no right, prying into Susan's past.'

'Susan's past is what's affecting our present,' said Kate.

A picture crashed from the wall and the doors of the glass-fronted book-case flew open, shattering the glass.

Maggie screamed, and Jon and Nick jumped to their feet.

'Now or never,' thought Kate. She picked up the drawing book from the table. 'Look at this, all of you!' She held the book up, turning the pages so they could see the beautifully detailed drawings.

A drawing of Jon's wrecked room.

A drawing of Kate crashing from her bike in a busy road.

Jack Carter and Nick on the steps, with the heavy flower pot flying towards Nick's head.

A gorilla-like Nick holding a man high in the air.

A dark monstrous shape bearing Maggie to the ground.

An exploding coffee-pot.

'They're drawings of things that happened to us,' said Nick.

'I think they're drawings that *made* things happen to us,' said Kate. 'They help to concentrate her mind.'

'But that's *Chrissie's* drawing book,' said Jon.

'That's right,' said Kate. 'Come and meet the enemy!'

Suddenly the windows flew open. Wind and rain rushed in to the room. As Kate made for the door Susan tried to hold her back.

'Kate, you mustn't, it's too dangerous. You don't know the risks . . .'

Kate pulled away. 'I've got a pretty good idea. And it's got to be dealt with hasn't it? We can't go on like this, it'll destroy us all.' She turned to her father. 'Dad, all of you, please, just trust me.'

Jack looked around the room, at his wife, his ex-wife and his two sons. 'All right, Kate,' he said. 'We'll come.'

Kate led the little party out of the room and up the stairs. The whole house seemed to be shaking now, doors slamming, windows shattering. Climbing the stairs was like fighting your way against a Force-Ten gale.

Chrissie's room was just next to the main bedroom. With the rest of the party clustered behind her, Kate forced open the door. Chrissie was sitting bolt upright in her bed, eyes staring, mouth open in a silent scream.

All around her toys, clothes, books, ornaments swirled through the air, caught up in a whirlpool of psychic energy.

'Jon's tornado,' thought Kate, 'Something like this must have trashed his room.'

Kate took a step into the room. All the others, even Susan, seemed unable to move.

Chrissie stared straight ahead, face distorted, dark eyes enormous, glowing . . .

Suddenly Kate realised that it wasn't triumph that was twisting Chrissie's face. It was fear.

124

Chrissie was as frightened as they were, the helpless victim of powers she couldn't possibly control. She forced her way forward, borne on a wave of affection for the terrified little figure in the bed. Somehow she reached the bedside, leaned over and picked Chrissie up, hugging her tight. 'There, there, Chrissie, it's all right, it's all right . . .'

The little body was tense and rigid at first, but gradually it relaxed. As it did so the energy storm died down, the swirling objects dropped to the ground and the house became quiet again.

Chrissie woke up and began to cry, normal childish sobs.

Then, astonishingly, she said, 'Kate? Kate, I was frightened. I want Mummy.'

'It's all right,' said Kate. 'Mummy's here.'

TWELVE

'Let me get this straight,' said Jack. 'Are you telling me little Chrissie *made* all these things happen? The accidents and everything?'

Kate saw the pain in Susan's face and shook her head. 'Chrissie didn't make anything happen, not really. We did it to ourselves. Chrissie just took what we gave her.'

Jon leaned forward, eyes gleaming eagerly. 'It's called psycho-telepathic amplification – I found a similar case in one of my books. Chrissie picks up emotional readings from the people around her. She finds violent emotions really terrifying, and since she hardly ever talks . . .'

'Hardly ever *talked*,' said Kate. 'She's started again now.'

Jon nodded. 'Anyway, the fears and emotions were all bottled up inside her and somehow she magnified them. The negative emotions took her over – *that's* what made things happen.'

'She can turn thoughts into reality,' said Kate. 'I thought about trashing Jon's room – and it was trashed. He thought about my brake cables snapping – and they snapped.' She looked at her father. 'Someone has a quick impulse to chuck a

126

stone flowerpot – suddenly it's flying through the air.'

'I hardly touched it,' protested Jack.

'I daresay you didn't,' said Kate. 'But with Chrissie involved, it's the thought that counts.'

'I don't see why I got attacked,' said Maggie.

'Nor do I,' said Jack. 'Surely no one can have been having bad thoughts about you, Maggie.'

'I should hope not!'

'That's why my row with that Kevin turned so bad,' Jack went on. 'I wanted to kick his backside and ended up nearly cutting his throat.'

Susan came into the room. 'Chrissie's asleep again.' Susan looked round the room and her eyes filled with tears. 'I'm sorry, I know I should have said something . . .'

Jon looked at her in astonishment. 'You knew it was Chrissie all along?'

'In a way. I suppose I was afraid to face it. Things have happened before . . .'

'That's why Kevin was so frightened, wasn't it?' said Kate.

Susan nodded and Jack led her to the sofa. 'Better tell us about it, love.'

'Kevin began drinking when Chrissie was very small,' said Susan. 'He was noisy and abusive. Violent, sometimes. That's when Chrissie stopped talking. Soon after that, things started happening. A slate came off the roof – it grazed Kevin's head. The toaster blew up and gave him an electric shock. A tree branch came down in the park. His car brakes failed on a steep hill. Whenever Kevin upset me, something happened to him. He got scared in the end and just ran out on us. After the divorce he reappeared, started asking me for money. He said if I didn't give it to him he'd get Chrissie taken away. He said she was a dangerous freak, they'd put her into some kind of institution.'

'But if you suspected what was happening, why on earth didn't you say something?' demanded Jon. 'Someone could have been killed, just because you kept quiet. Even if Chrissie wasn't doing it on purpose . . .'

'I know,' said Susan miserably. 'But I just didn't dare.'

Jack put his arm round her. 'Why didn't you tell me?'

'I was afraid you'd run out on me too. Not everyone wants to take on a mother and child – and a child with Chrissie's problems . . .'

'You underestimated him,' said Kate. 'Dad's no saint, but he's no Kevin either. He doesn't run out on people. He won't let you down, Susan. None of us will.'

'Suppose these terrible things go on happening?'

'I don't see why they need to. Not now Chrissie's talking again. Besides, the secret's out now, and we all know the score. Chrissie just plays back what we give her – so all we've got to do is to stop giving her so much violence and anger. We'll work it out.'

Maggie had been listening to all this with a baffled air. Suddenly she stood up. 'I think I ought to be moving. Are you coming, Nick?'

'No, I think I'll stay on for a bit Mum, help clear up. Might even sleep here if that's okay?'

He looked at his father who said gruffly, 'Fine by me.'

'Did I tell you I'm going back to college, Dad? Going to do a conversion course, change to studying law.'

'You're kidding!'

'Your mate Charlie Salter gave me the idea, when I had my spot of bother. You should have seen how he chivvied those cops about! Imagine annoying the police and getting paid for it . . .'

Maggie was looking left out, so Kate said, 'I'll see you to the door, Mum.'

Maggie said her goodbyes and Kate took her into the hall and helped her into her coat. Maggie paused on the front doorstep.

'Are you sure you're all right here, Kate? I mean with everything that's been happening . . . You can't be sure it's all going to stop. Even if it does, life with your father's never going to be easy.'

'I suppose not,' said Kate.

'You could move in with me,' said Maggie suddenly. 'I mean, now you're grown up, we could get to know each other better. We could be friends.'

Kate looked at her in amazement. Maggie was quite serious. She looked anxious, as if she really wanted Kate to agree. It suddenly struck Kate that Maggie might actually be lonely.

Kate thought about the offer for a moment. A comfortable, civilised life with Maggie in her elegant flat. It would be very different. Maggie could be difficult but Kate was confident that she could handle her. And she'd only have one person to deal with, not Jack and Nick and Jon and Susan and Chrissie and all their problems. All the endless upsets of Carter family life.

But then, how could they possibly manage without her?

There was no choice really. The idea of life with Maggie just didn't seem real any more. Her home was here.

'No thanks, Mum,' said Kate gently. 'I think I'll soldier on. Thanks for the offer, though.'

She gave Maggie a quick hug, kissed her on the cheek and watched her trot off down the street in her neat, smart suit towards her neat, smart car.

Then she closed the door and turned back into the house.

On a sudden impulse Kate went upstairs to take another look at Chrissie. The room had been tidied and Chrissie was curled up in bed, dark hair contrasting with the white pillowslip. As Kate bent over her, Chrissie opened her eyes and smiled. 'Kate,' she said sleepily. 'Nice Kate . . .'

She drifted back off to sleep. The room felt peaceful and calm.

'Well, so far so good,' thought Kate. 'Let's hope we can keep it up.'

She went downstairs to join the family.

SAGITTARIUS – MISSING
23 November–21st December

Employment prospects loom on the horizon but you are right to be apprehensive. Be careful – things aren't always what they seem.

Fifteen-year-old Andrea, usually known as Andi, gets a job in a crafts shop in the shopping mall. The proprietor seems a little strange but Andi's happy enough. She does, however, feel that she's being watched and finds out that two missing teenagers had previously worked in the shop. And then, when she's working late, the lights go out. Andi panics and runs out of the shop but too late – the shopping mall's on fire and Andi is trapped . . .

CAPRICORN – CAPRICORN'S CHILDREN
22nd December–19th January

A relative is behaving strangely but act with caution – this is a dangerous time for you both.

Jan becomes concerned about her brother, Jimmy, who seems to have become withdrawn and quiet. Then she discovers articles in his room published by the Church of Capricorn and, not wanting to confront Jimmy directly, goes to the church herself. The preacher there is a charismatic man but Jan is suspicious about the church's influence over her brother – and then she hears that the congregation plan to kill themselves in a mass suicide. Can she save her brother?

AQUARIUS – TRAPPED
20th January–18th February

An argument with someone you love brings trouble crashing down like a bolt from the blue.

Following a family argument, two teenagers, Lucy and Alan, go to the cathedral one night to explore. That same evening, their father, a pilot with the RAF, is involved in night exercises with his squadron. But something goes badly wrong; a plane hits the cathedral tower and the cathedral's bell smashes to the ground – trapping Lucy inside . . .

PISCES – REVENGE
19th February–20th March

*There is a price to be paid for everything in this
life and your payments are now overdue.*

While slightly drunk, Danny steals a car and goes
joy-riding with his girlfriend, Jo. But there's an
accident; Danny hits a girl in the street but,
terrified, he drives off. Jo, too drunk at the time
to realise what was happening, becomes fasci-
nated by the victim of the accident, Samantha,
and goes to visit the now paralysed girl in
hospital, concealing her true involvement. But
then, as events reach a dramatic climax, Jo discovers too late that Samantha has a thirst for
vengeance . . .

GEMINI – SLICED APART
21st May–20th June

*Avoid confrontations with relatives – there could
be unpleasant and unexpected consequences.*

Nina has never forgiven her twin, Gemma, for
being born first, believing (wrongly) that Gemma
is her parents' favourite. Then Nina finds that
the boy she has idolised, Daniel, has started going
out with Gemma. Overcome with jealousy, Nina
begins to think of ways to get rid of her sister –
and forges a terrible friendship with a murderer.
Will Gemma be safe?

TAURUS – MIRROR IMAGE
21st April–20th May

*A new friendship will bring delights but
also troubles – tread carefully. Someone looks
to you to give them strength, but you will need
to be brave.*

Fifth-former Dianne soon makes friends with the
new girl, Jeannette. But soon Dianne and her
other friends find that Jeannette has strange
mood changes, not to mention the unpleasant
things that sometimes happen around her – a
boy's hand is trapped in a locker, Dianne's dog
is killed and Dianne's baby brother is found with
a jar of angry wasps. The friendship continues
until an afternoon's boating trip turns into a
near-disaster and Dianne begins to feel that there
is something quite evil about Jeannette . . .

CANCER – BLACK DEATH
21st June–20th July

*The sun in Saturn suggests an ominous turn
of events. The distant past may come back to
haunt you and you should act with caution.
A good turn may have unexpected and
unpleasant consequences.*

A family trip to Maris Caulfield, a village which
was wiped out during the plague in the four-
teenth century, turns into a nightmare for Janie
Hyde. Exploring the village, she discovers a
cottage bearing a plaque to the people who lived
and died there during the plague years – including
a Jayne Hyde. Janie starts to get 'flashbacks',
going back in time to watch as Jayne Hyde's life
crumbles as those around her die of the plague.
But it seems that Jayne's spirit is trying to take
over Janie's body and Janie's own life is now in
danger . . .

Nicholas Pine

TERROR ACADEMY: STUDENT BODY

Abby Wilder is a bright and popular senior, a cheerleader and straight-A student. And the victim of an attacker who clearly intended to kill her!

While the police search desperately for clues, Abby's memory of the attack fades completely. But not the strange visions that seem to be warning her: this killer has rampaged before – and is about to strike again . . .

Also available in the Terror Academy *series*

Lights Out
Stalker
Sixteen Candles
Spring Break
The New Kid
Night School
Science Project
Summer School
The Prom
The In Crowd

A Selected List of Fiction from Mammoth

While every effort is made to keep prices low, it is sometimes necessary to increase prices at short notice. Mandarin Paperbacks reserves the right to show new retail prices on covers which may differ from those previously advertised in the text or elsewhere.

The prices show below were correct at the time of going to press.

☐ 7497 0978 2	**Trial of Anna Cotman**	Vivien Alcock	£2.99
☐ 7497 1510 3	**A Map of Nowhere**	Gillian Cross	£2.99
☐ 7497 1066 7	**The Animals of Farthing Wood**	Colin Dann	£3.99
☐ 7497 0914 6	**Follyfoot**	Monica Dickens	£2.99
☐ 7497 0184 6	**The Summer House Loon**	Anne Fine	£2.99
☐ 7497 0443 8	**Fast From the Gate**	Michael Hardcastle	£2.50
☐ 7497 1784 X	**Listen to the Dark**	Maeve Henry	£2.99
☐ 7497 0136 6	**I Am David**	Anne Holm	£3.50
☐ 7497 1473 5	**Charmed Life**	Diana Wynne Jones	£3.50
☐ 7497 1664 9	**Hiding Out**	Elizabeth Laird	£2.99
☐ 7497 0791 7	**The Ghost of Thomas Kempe**	Penelope Lively	£2.99
☐ 7497 0634 1	**Waiting for Anya**	Michael Morpurgo	£2.99
☐ 7497 0831 X	**The Snow Spider**	Jenny Nimmo	£2.99
☐ 7497 0412 8	**Voices of Danger**	Alick Rowe	£2.99
☐ 7497 0410 1	**Space Demons**	Gillian Rubinstein	£2.99
☐ 7497 0656 2	**Journey of 1000 Miles**	Ian Strachan	£2.99
☐ 7497 0796 8	**Kingdom by the Sea**	Robert Westall	£2.99

All these books are available at your bookshop or newsagent, or can be ordered direct from the address below. Just tick the title you want and fill in the form below.

Cash Sales Department, PO Box 5, Rushden, Northants NN10 6YX.
Fax: 0933 410321 : Phone 0933 410511.

Please send cheque, payable to 'Reed Book Services Ltd', or postal order for purchase price quoted and allow the following for postage and packing:

£1.00 for the first book. 50p for the second; **FREE POSTAGE AND PACKING FOR THREE BOOKS OR MORE PER ORDER.**

NAME (Block letters) . . . .

ADDRESS . . . .

. . . .

☐ I enclose my remittance for . . . .

☐ I wish to pay by Access/Visa Card Number

Expiry Date

Signature . . . .

Please quote our reference: MAND